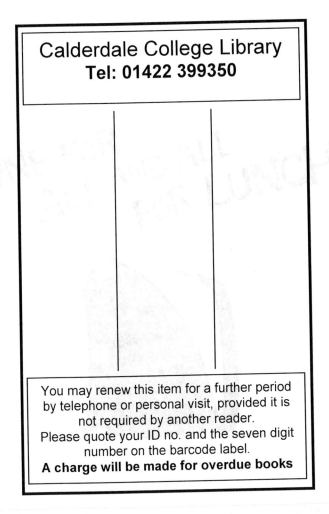

Calderdale College Library
Tel: 01422 399350

You may renew this item for a further period
by telephone or personal visit, provided it is
not required by another reader.
Please quote your ID no. and the seven digit
number on the barcode label.
A charge will be made for overdue books

The Jiggy McCue books can be read in any order, but to get the most out of them (Jiggy and Co are a wee bit older in each one) we suggest you read them in the following order:

Visit Michael Lawrence's website:
www.wordybug.com

And find loads of Jiggy fun at:
www.jiggymccue.co.uk

JIGGY McCUE STORIES

ONE FOR ALL AND ALL FOR LUNCH

MICHAEL LAWRENCE

ORCHARD BOOKS

ORCHARD BOOKS
338 Euston Road, London NW1 3BH
Orchard Books Australia
Level 17/207 Kent Street, Sydney, NSW 2000

First published in 2009 by Orchard Books

ISBN 978 1 84616 956 4

Text © Michael Lawrence 2009
Illustrations © Steve May 2009

1 2 3 4 5 6 7 8 9 10

Printed in Great Britain

Orchard Books is a division of Hachette Children's Books,
an Hachette UK company.

www.hachette.co.uk

For
Rob the Rock God
&
Janie the Witch

CONTENTS

Stories by the Three Musketeers plus One

THE BOGEY MAN

by

Jiggy McCue

Question. Where do nose bogeys come from? Answer. They're bits of brain chipping off. That's what my dad says anyway. Mum says that in his case that explains a lot.

I mention this because of the bogey man, but I didn't know about him the night I lay awake listening to Eejit Atkins snoring. Why was I listening to Eejit snoring when he lives next door? Because it was summer, and warm, and I had to have the window open or I'd have melted all over the mattress, and the little Cossack had decided to sleep in a tent in his back garden. I would have gone to the window and yelled something like 'Shut it, Atkins, you twonk, some people are trying to sleep here!', but I didn't want to wake other neighbours who can sleep through snoring but not yells. I'm considerate that way.

Because I'd turned and tossed so much in the night I felt pretty manky next morning. Manky makes me slow, so when Pete and Angie called for me I wasn't ready. I told them to go on without me, which they did, the traitors. When I finally left the house (because Mum shoved me off the front step) who should I bump into dragging his school bag past my gate but the King of Snores himself.

'Hiya, Jig,' Atkins said. 'I got summin' ta show ya!'

'Yeah, and I've got summin' to show you,' I said, raising my fist to his eyes, then thumping his shoulder with it.

'What's this, McCue?!' bawled a depressingly familiar voice from behind us. 'You know the rules on bullying, boy!'

I turned. Mr Rice, my Pointless Exercises teacher, who, O Joy, had recently moved into our street with Miss Weeks, the Deputy Head. He was jogging to school as usual in his stupid red tracksuit.

'Atkins asked for it,' I said.

'He asked to be bullied?!' Rice bawled. (Rice always bawls, even when whispering.) 'Somehow I doubt that!'

I gave Atkins the Mean Eye. 'Tell him,' I said.

And to my amazement, Eejit got it for once

without it being written down for him in large slow capitals.

'Jig's right, sir, I arsed fer it.'

The Ricipops drew level with us and started running on the spot.

'Well whether you did or not,' he said, 'whether you *deserved* it or not, the next time your neighbour feels like playing rough he'd better pick on someone his own size – me, for instance!'

'You're not my size,' I said. 'You're twice my size.'

Even a sporty nut-job like Mr Rice had to accept this. 'Yes!' he said. 'Pity! But if I see behaviour of this sort on the way to school again, you can count on being in some pretty hot water, lad! Got it?!'

He didn't wait for a reply, which was probably just as well because I couldn't think of one that wouldn't get me hanged, drawn, quartered and sold in bits at the next Save Our Lousy School car boot.

'Now see what you've done,' I said to Atkins as Rice jogged off.

'I din't do nuffin',' Atkins said.

'I'll tell you what you did,' I said. 'You snored all night long and kept me awake from the moment my head hit the pillow to the moment I woke up.'

'Sorry, mate,' he said. 'It's me sinuses. I'm all blocked up. Me mum fort sleepin' aata doors might clear me 'ead. 'Ere, lemme me show ya this fing I made.' He felt for something in his jacket pocket.

'Not interested,' I said, and stormed on ahead.

'Nah, but you'll like this!' he yelled after me.

'I won't! Go boil your head! That'll help your stinking sinuses!'

Even though I didn't want to know, I saw what Eejit wanted to show me during the day's first lesson, when Mr Dakin stepped out for a minute, probably to bang his head against the brick wall he was always going on about. I only looked because other kids were crowding round, and I like to know what's happening in the world. Eejit – the prat – had made this little box that looked like a coffin, and when he lifted the lid there was this man-shaped model inside. The man was greeny-brown and all knobbly, and he didn't have much of a face, and he was nude, and Atkins, because he was Atkins, had made it *absolutely clear* that he was a man, if you know what I mean. This got a few laughs, even from the girls, but even I had to admit that it was quite funny when he took the man out of the box and made him dance.

'What's it made of, Eej – rubber?' someone asked.

'Bogeys,' Atkins said.

'What?'

'Me bogeys. From me 'ooter.'

'*What!*' said everyone, stepping back a group pace.

He then told us that he'd been lugging bogeys out of his nose for about a year. Hauling them in strips sometimes, but other times just in little knots, adding them to the rest like new blobs of chewed gum. He said the best bogey time was first thing in the morning because his nose was almost always blocked up then, and he'd been storing them in shrink-wrap to keep them moist, and last night, in his tent in the garden, by torchlight, he'd shaped the little man to go in the coffin he'd made some other time.

There were quite a few shudders and groans as he told us this, and absolutely no one wanted to touch the little bogey man. Some flew back to their desks in disgust, including me and Pete, which was just as well because as we got there Dakin barged in demanding to know why half the class were out of their seats and not working on the ultra-boring rubbish he'd told us to get on with.

'Because Atkins is a dickhead,' Pete explained.

'What's he done now?' our beloved form tutor asked.

'Ask him,' said Pete.

'Atkins, what have you done?' Face-Ache asked Eejit.

Before Eejit could reply, several others answered for him, but as they all spoke at once Mr D couldn't make sense of it. He marched to Eejit's desk and demanded to be shown whatever it was everyone was so fascinated by. Atkins showed him.

'What's this…*obscenity* supposed to represent?' Dakin enquired.

'It's me bogey man,' said Eejit.

'Your what?'

'He made it with his own bogeys,' Kelly Ironmonger said.

Dakin stared at the thing like he didn't believe what he'd just heard or was looking at. Then it seemed to click because he said, 'Atkins, there's something seriously wrong with you.'

Eejit grinned up at him. He knew this was true

and it didn't bother him one bit. He slotted the bogey man back in the coffin and jammed the lid on.

Face-Ache held his hand out. He didn't need to speak. Even a kid as dim as Atkins knew what the silent hand meant. He handed the coffin over. He wasn't so chirpy now. He'd been looking forward to showing his bogey man off to other kids at break.

Later. Tail end of yet another yawny school day. We were packing up in the room where Mrs Porterhouse had been failing to teach us Geography when Mr Staples (who fails to teach us RE) stuck his head round the door on a stick and asked me to go to the staff room.

'What, before going home?' I asked suspiciously.

'Before would be good,' he replied.

'Why, what have I done now?'

'I have no idea, just passing on the message.'

'Do as you're told please, Jiggy,' Mrs Porterhouse said.

'What, and break my unblemished record?' I zapped back.

But I went to the staff room to see what trouble

I was in for the gadzillionth time in my stunning school career, and as it happened – woh, put out the flags! – I wasn't in *any* for a change. When I knocked, someone yelled 'Come!', and I looked in and saw a batch of teachers flopped in chairs or stuffing work in briefcases or shopping bags to take home and burn.

'I was told to come here,' I said.

'Why?' asked one of the ones I only know by sight.

'Not a clue.'

'Ah, Jiggy. It was me that sent for you.' This was Mr Dent, Lord of Resistant Materials. 'Mr Dakin asked me to give you this.' He held out Eejit's little coffin.

'Not mine,' I said.

'No, I know, but Eejit had to stay behind for some reason, and he asked Mr Dakin to ask you to take it home for him, and as Mr Dakin had to rush off to his Vegetarian Sushi course at the College the task fell to me to make sure it fell to you. Does that make any sense at all?'

'I might have to write it down and go over it slowly with my tongue between my teeth,' I said.

But I took the box in the finger and thumb of one hand.

'Why so wary of handling it?' Mr Dent asked.

'It's Atkins's.'

'Oh. Yeah.'

I put the coffin in my pocket – carefully, so it wouldn't open. Of all the things I might want to carry about my person, something crafted out of Eejit Atkins's bogeys was not up there with the frontrunners.

When I got home I went up to my room and shoved the little box under my bed. Then I forgot about it till we'd started tea and the phone rang and Mum picked up. 'It's Ralph,' she said.

I snatched the phone. 'Whaddayawant?' I said to it.

'Did yer pick me bogey man up from da starf room?' Eejit enquired daintily.

'Yeah.'

'Kin I come raand fer 'im then?'

'No, I'm having me tea.'

'When then?'

'When I've finished.'

'When'll that be?'

19

'When I've *finished*!'

I hung up.

'You're not very nice to Ralph, are you?' Mum said.

'I don't want to encourage him. Encourage him and he'll be round here all the time, like a rash.'

After tea I went upstairs and felt under my bed for the coffin. I couldn't feel it right away so I had to grope around for it. When I found it I pulled it out – another finger and thumb job – only to find that the lid was off and that it was empty. It must have tipped over when I chucked it under here, I thought, sticking my bum in the air and peering into the fluffy darkness. I couldn't see much apart from a stack of junk and old clothes, so I dug out the little torch I'd got in a Christmas cracker, and flashed it around. It wasn't a bright beam, but it was bright enough to show no sign of the little man. Just then I heard my latest favourite ringtone (specially chosen because it really annoys my parents). I backed out from under the bed and grabbed my phone. Eejit again.

'How'd you get this number?' I snapped. 'I only give it to people I want to hear from, which doesn't include you.'

'Garrett give it me,' he said.

'I'll be having stern words with him,' I said.

'Kin I come raand nah?'

'No.'

'Why?'

'Cos I say so.'

'So when?'

'When I say so.'

I clicked off. And then I thought, Why did I lie to Eejit Atkins? Why didn't I just say I couldn't find his crummy bogey man? Maybe it was because I was annoyed about this that I didn't go back under the bed and look further. 'Better things to do with my time,' I said aloud. Then I looked around for something to do. I couldn't find anything, so I went downstairs to watch TV. No point to that either as it turned out. The Golden Oldies were hogging it. So I started my homework. Yes, I know, you're *really* at a loose end if you do your homework without being ordered to by a snarling adult.

Later, I was sitting at the kitchen table (doodling in the margins of my History exercise book instead of writing the historical rubbish Mr Hurley had told us to) when I heard this unholy kerfuffle of dogs barking and little kids wailing from somewhere outside. I got up and went to the window, but there was nothing to see from there, so I went to the front door. As I opened it I felt something soft slip between my ankles – our cat, Stallone. He must also have wanted to investigate the racket, but was too chicken to do it on his own. 'Stick with me, cat,' I said, and led the way up the path.

At the gate, I leaned over the top and Stallone stuck his head between the uprights to see what was happening. The howling was from kids at the windows of nearby houses. The barking was from dogs staring towards the streetlamp on the pavement across from us, which at first I thought must be casting the shadow that was getting them all agitated. It was some shadow. Huge, menacing, with a hunched back, hands raised like claws, mouth open in a silent howl or snarl. I looked down at Stallone. His fur was up. I felt the back of my neck. So was mine.

And then I saw who the shadow belonged to. He was standing so close to the wall on the other side of the road that Stallone and I were probably the only ones who could see him apart from the dogs. He was a very small man. I mean *incredibly* small. Can't have been more than forty centimetres high. And he had nothing on, nothing at all, even socks. The enormous shadow that was terrifying the sprogs and dogs of the neighbourhood ran all the way back to his tiny feet, but it wasn't made by the streetlamp. It spread out from him without any light behind him, and just...grew. He wasn't crouching or trying to look fierce either. He was just standing there. The shadow was making its own shape, without its owner's help.

'Oh, no,' I muttered.

I said this because I've seen a whole truckload of weird stuff in my life, met a barrelful of whacko characters, experienced great twitching bunches of unnatural doings, and I'd had enough of them. I wanted a normal boring life like everyone else. So I turned my back on the street.

'Come on, Stallone. Inside.'

He didn't need telling twice. He was indoors before I was.

'What's all that wailing and barking?' my

23

mother asked as I closed the front door.

'What wailing and barking?'

'From outside.'

'I can't hear anything.'

'Oh, you must.'

'Is that an order?'

She sighed. 'I think it's time you went to bed, my lad.'

'I don't.'

'Don't argue, Jiggy, you know the rule on school nights.'

'It's not a school night.'

'It's Wednesday. Therefore it's a school night.'

'It's Wednesday,' I agreed. 'But I don't do school at night.'

'Don't be silly, you know what I mean.'

Of course I knew what she meant, but winding my mother up is one of my life's few pleasures. I went into the kitchen. She followed me.

'What's this?' she said, staring at the table.

'It's the kitchen table,' I said, hoping to jog her memory.

'Is that your homework?'

'It's *some* of my homework. Why?'

'You're doing it without being told to?'

'I was really keen to get on with it. Then the wailing and barking started.'

'I thought you couldn't hear the wailing and barking.'

'What wailing and barking?'

Just as I finished shoving my books in my bag so I could forget they existed for a year or two, the kitchen phone rang. I walked past it. Mum could answer it. It wouldn't be for me.

She answered it. 'It's for you,' she said.

'Who is it?'

'Ralph.'

'Tell him to get lost.'

She slapped the phone into my hand. 'Speak to him!'

I reluctantly put the phone to my face. 'What now?' I growled.

'Kin I come raand yet?' Eejit asked in his whiny little voice.

'No.'

I hung up. I didn't need to see him now. His bogey man was no longer in my possession. He was out in the street, mysteriously alive and quite a bit bigger and scaring half the neighbourhood's pets and kids. Not my problem any more.

Or so I thought.

It was another warm night, so once again I would have to leave my window open. This meant that Eejit's snores from the garden next door would keep me awake a second night. Or maybe not. I'd dug out the old electric fan from the spare room, where we kept all the stuff we didn't know what to do with. I plugged it in, hoping it still worked, because if I could cool the room down I'd be able to shut the window and get some peace. It did work, but not brilliantly, and it was very noisy, like there was something loose inside it. Still, I left it on and jumped into my PJs.

In bed I lay waiting for the room to cool, but the fan only threw a morsel of breeze my way – better than nothing but not enough to close the window. I listened to the fan for about half an hour until I decided to turn it off and see if Eejit was snoring. He was, and his snores were even more of a pain than the rattle of the fan, so I left the window open and turned the fan back on.

I must have slept eventually, because I definitely wasn't awake before I woke up somewhere around the middle of the night. It was one of those funny-unfunny wakings where your brain slowly drags itself up from the ditch and you realise where you are, even though your eyes are shut. Then you slide the old lids up a bit, and then, if you're Jiggy McCue, you see something in the moonlight that's flooding your room because you haven't drawn the curtains. Something that fires the same lids all the way up to your hairline and zings your eyeballs out on stalks as a cry of horror gargles in your throat.

All this occurred because of the hulking great shadow on the opposite wall. A shadow with a gaping mouth, hunched shoulders, hands raised like talons. Too terrified to wonder why I was seeing something so nightmarish while awake, I shot back against the wall and waited for my heart to claw its way back up from my knees by the scenic route. While I waited, the shadow stayed on the wall, moving a bit but not much, like it knew there were just so many menacing poses a shadow can do in profile. Sitting there, duvet in mouth, my

27

brown, knobbly, pretty ugly, and totally nude.

'How come you can cast a shadow from under a bed where there's no light?' I asked.

'It just seems to be something I can do,' he answered.

'And the scary shapes?'

'My shadow does them, not me.'

I got up and fetched Eejit's miniature coffin from where I'd left it on my chest of drawers.

'This is where you came from, right?'

'It's what I woke up in.'

'Woke up in? You weren't alive. How can something that's not alive wake up?'

He shrugged. A bogey fell off his shoulder.

'Mystery to me,' he said.

'Maybe it's the shape,' I said.

'Shape?'

'The human look. Maybe when all the boge...all the parts that made you were stuck together it was like putting a battery in something to make it work. And maybe you didn't come to life straight away because the battery had to charge itself up.'

'I have no idea what you're talking about,' he said.

'Makes two of us. Why are you bigger than you were in the box?'

'I've grown. Isn't that what life does to a person? Makes him grow?'

He had a point. In fact he had two, and the other one wasn't one I wanted to see.*

'Cover yourself up, will you?' I said. 'This is a respectable bedroom, in spite of what my mother says.'

'I haven't got anything to cover myself with.'

I opened a drawer in my chest (of drawers) and took out a perfectly ironed blue-and-white handkerchief. I unfolded it, made a small triangle, held it out to him.

'What do I do with this?' he asked.

'You put it round your middle, like a nappy.'

'I don't know how.'

'Course you do.'

'I don't. If you want me covered up, you'll have to do it.'

The thought of doing this did not make my night, but I gritted the McCue teeth, steered the triangled hanky under his miniature crotch, and pulled together the long bits that came round his hips.

---

* Like I said before, Atkins had made it absolutely clear that he was a bogey *man*, not a bogey woman.

'Hold these corners,' I said.

He held the corners while I grabbed the staple gun from my desk and stapled them together. Then I went to the bathroom to wash my hands.*

When I returned there was no sign of the little man. I closed the door.

'Where are you?' I whispered.

The top half of my duvet jumped, and there he was, sitting up in my bed, grinning ear to knobbly ear. 'Peek-a-boo!'

'Get out of there!' I hissed.

'But it's so nice in here.'

'I know it is. That's why I want you out.'

'You're no fun,' he said sulkily, sliding to the edge of the mattress and dropping to the carpet.

'How did you get back here from the street?' I asked then.

'I climbed up like I climbed down.'

'Climbed what?'

'That pole thing out there.'

I went to the window, looked out, saw what he meant. The drainpipe that runs past my window.

'Why did you come back anyway?'

'I didn't know where else to go.'

---

* Well, wouldn't you wash *your* hands if you'd been touching giant versions of someone else's bogeys?

'You could have gone off on your travels, scaring kids and animals wherever you went with your shadow.'

'I could, but...' He looked kind of embarrassed.

'But what?'

'A monster chased me.'

'Monster?'

'A fearsome beast that made a horrible loud noise, like...'

He gave me a demo. One of the dogs must have overcome its terror of the shadow and gone after him.

The bogey man spent the rest of the night under my bed. I would've preferred to be under it myself after he'd been in it, but there didn't seem to be any loose bogeys in there, so I chanced it.

Next morning he was up before I was, which was unfortunate because he'd been silently busy. I woke to find my room even more of a disaster area than usual. Looked like a bomb had been tossed through the window while I snoozed.

'What have you done?' I gasped, staring around.

'I was exploring,' he said.

'Exploring? Holy bogeys. My mother'll have

a fit if she sees this!'

A fist struck the outside of my door. 'Jig, are you up?' Talk about timing.

I leapt out of bed and kicked the bogey man under it just before Mum threw the door back.

'You'll be late for school,' she said from the threshold. 'Why you don't set your alarm, I'll never kn...'

Her mouth stopped flapping as her eyes focused. When she finally found her voice again, she cranked it up to ask what I'd been doing in there. I told her I'd been tidying up.

'Tidying *up*?' she said. 'It's more of a mess than ever!'

'I'd just started. I'll finish later, after school. Thanks for reminding me about that, by the way. School, I mean.'

I slammed the door on her nose.

Before setting off for school I told the bogey man to stay under the bed till I got home. He wasn't happy about this.

'What will I do all day?'

'Nothing,' I said. 'And make my room any worse while I'm away and you're back down the drainpipe – and I don't mean *climbing* down.'

Outside I met Pete and Angie and headed off with them, like I do every day that they bother to wait for me. After a while Angie asked why I was so quiet.

'WHO, ME?' I shouted, for the world next door to hear.

'If you're in one of your moods, you can go on your own,' she said.

'What do you mean, one of my moods? I don't get moods.'

She curled her lip. 'Don't get moods! Oh yeah, right.'

'I don't, do I, Pete?'

'If you say so,' he muttered.

'No, hang on,' I said, pulling them both to a halt. 'Let's get this straight. I do not get moods. OK?'

'OK,' said Angie.

'Mm,' said Pete.

'I don't!' I said.

'Riiiiight,' said Angie, moving forward again. Pete kicked a tin can and got in step with her.

'I DO NOT GET MOODS!' I bawled after them.

They didn't answer. We went the rest of the way

in silence. I was in a right mood by the time we got to school.

The first person I looked for in the playground was Atkins in case he'd beaten me to our personal palace of excellence for a change. I needed to tell him about his bogey man coming alive and growing, and get him to take him off my hands and out of my room. There was no sign of him.

'Anyone know where Atkins is?' Mr Dakin asked just two names in at Registration.

'Probably just late,' someone said.

'If he is, he's in trouble,' said Dakin.

By the end of Reg, Atkins still hadn't showed, and he carried on not showing. The first time I ever wanted to see him and he wasn't around. There was no one else I could talk to about the bogey man either. Normally Pete and Angie were the first people I would turn to with stuff like this, but after their Jiggy's-in-a-mood stunt on the way to school I didn't want to talk to them about anything. I didn't even eat with them at lunchtime, just lurked nearby getting heartburn from my terrible packed lunch while they happily swapped theirs on our private bench in the Concrete Garden.

'How's the mood coming?' Angie hollered at one point.

'Bog off!' I hollered back.

'You're very aggressive lately, McCue!' said Mr Rice, who just happened to be bouncing a ball behind me.

It was on the tip of my tongue to ask him if he wanted to make something of it, but I managed not to.

Eventually, after what felt like three days packed into one, it was home time. I dashed off without waiting for anyone. When I got to my street I thought of going straight to Eejit's, but I knew I wouldn't get my daily bicky fix there, so I went to mine instead.

The kitchen would have been my first stop if I hadn't heard a strangled wail from the cupboard under the stairs. I pulled the door back and saw Stallone hiding behind the vacuum cleaner. He looked so terrified that I guessed he'd gone into the cupboard and tried to close the door behind him.

'What's the prob, mad mog?' I asked politely.

'Ssssss!' (Catese for 'Take a flying leap, McCue.')

I heard a sound from the kitchen. It was too

early for Mum to be home, and Dad was working afternoons at the council tip, so it could only be one person. I shut the door on Stallone and crept to the kitchen. What I saw when I looked into the kitchen made my jaw drop to my bellybutton. Nothing that could be moved in there was where it should be. Cupboards and drawers were open, and there was food everywhere. I mean *everywhere*.

'OK, where are you?' I said.

Something moved in the fridge. I hauled the door back. And there he was, squatting between the low-fat spreads and the yogurts, tucking into a chicken leg. It must have been black in there before I opened the door, but it either hadn't bothered him or he could see in the dark. The cold can't have put him out much either, because he grinned happily when he saw me.

'Food is good,' he said.

I snatched the chicken leg off him. 'Explain!'

'Explain what?'

'All this.'

'I was just looking at a few things. Tasting some of them.'

'Terrific. I'll never get it straight before Mum gets in!'

'Jiggy?'

I whirled. It was she. In the doorway. She'd got this talk-of-the-devil thing down to a fine art.

'You're early,' I said, jerking the chicken leg behind me and popping it back in the fridge.

My mother came further in, staring wildly about her. 'What…what…what?' she said.

'Just what I was thinking,' I said. 'What, what, what?, I thought.'

'You mean you don't know?'

'Know what?'

'About this…mess!'

'How could I? Just got in myself. I thought it was you.'

'Me?'

'Thought you must've got an afternoon off and started spring-cleaning, even though it's nowhere near spring.'

'No. I'm only home this early because I was offered a lift.'

'Oh. Well there's only one thing it can mean then.'

'What's that?'

'We've been vandalised.'

'Vandalised? Are you saying that someone broke *in* and did all this?'

'Well, they weren't invited in to do it. Not by me anyway.'

Her eyes popped. 'Jig! They might still be in the house!'

'Good thought,' I said. 'I'll go and check, shall I?'

'You'll stay right here!'

She grabbed the rolling pin she never uses and stormed towards the hall. I waited till she was halfway up the stairs before turning back to the half-open fridge. I looked in.

The bogey man wasn't there!

I was still gaping into the fridge when something dropped on my head. I felt in my hair. Pulled out a small rubbery blob. I looked up. There he was, clinging to the ceiling like Spiderman.

'Look at me, all upside down!' he said.

'Come down from there!' I said, flicking the bogey in my hand at the bread bin.

He dropped from the ceiling to the floor – 'Weeeeeeee!' – and bounced a bit. I needed to hide him before Mum got back. But where? Couldn't put him back in the fridge, she might open it. Ditto any of the cupboards. My school bag? Yes! I darted out to the hall for it, tipped everything out, kicked it all into a corner, held the bag open.

'Get in!'

The bogey man frowned at the bag. 'Why?'

'You've got to hide!'

He looked up at me with a pained expression. 'Are you ashamed of me?'

'Yes! Get in!'

He sniffed sadly, but climbed in and sat down. Even sitting, his head was higher than the top of the bag.

'Make yourself smaller.'

'I can't.'

I heard Mum's feet coming downstairs and forced the rubbery head lower, tucked in a rubbery arm, zipped up the bag, and was innocently wiping my hands on the tea towel as she came in.

'No one up there,' she said.

'Relief,' I said.

'We'd better call the police.'

'The police? You don't want to do that.'

She gave me one of her Deeply Suspicious looks.

'Jiggy, are you sure you don't know anything about this?'

'How could I? Like I said, I've only just got in.'

'Because if I find out that you do...'

'I swear. On my mother's life.'

'Well, someone's been here to make all this mess.'

'It was probably just a one-off,' I said.

'One-off?'

'Somebody having a lark.'

'Breaking into a private house and vandalising it for a *lark*?'

'Yeah. We don't want to get carried away and make a heavy thing of it or next thing you know we'll be in the local rag, and we've had enough of that, I think, don't you?'*

While she got stuck into a detailed survey of the devastation, I snuck upstairs, bumping my school bag after me to teach the bogey man a lesson.

In my room, I speed-dialled Eejit. 'Where the hell have you been all day?' I snarled when he answered.

''Ere,' he said.

''Ere?'

---

* For other McCue appearances in the local paper, see *The Curse of the Poltergoose* and *Kid Swap*.

'At 'ome.'

'Why?'

'Din't fancy school.'

'Who does?' I said. 'But we go. Usually. I wanted to see you because I have something of yours that you've got to take back.'

'Wossat 'en?'

'What do you mean, "wossat 'en"? You know wossat. Your twonking bogey man, that's wossat.'

'Oh...yeah...forgot abaat 'im.'

'Atkins, you half-baked cretin. How could you forget him? You were pestering me for him all last night!'

'Wuz I?'

I clutched my head. You can get more sense out of the graffiti on a ruined wall than Eejit Atkins sometimes. No, always.

'I'm coming round!' I said.

I clicked off, grabbed my bag, which was wriggling a bit, and headed downstairs again.

'Going next door,' I said to Mum, who'd already started on the kitchen.

'No you're not,' she said. 'You're going to help me put this kitchen straight.'

'Me? But I didn't do it.'

'So you say.'

'I didn't!'

'Well neither did I, and I'm expected to tidy it, so why shouldn't you help?'

'I'm a kid,' I said. 'You're a mother. Sorting kitchens is mothers' work. Unwritten law.'

'Oh yes, and who wrote *that*, I wonder?'

'Nobody. It's unwritten. I gotta go see Eejit.'

'See him later. Right now you're with me, and when we've got this cleaned up, you can get to work on your room.'

Knowing when I was beaten – 'Just a *minute* then!' – I stomped back upstairs with my bag, shoved it under my bed, told it to keep quiet, and went down again to help Boss Woman as ordered.

When my dad called me for tea, the bogey man, in his hanky-nappy, was strolling around on top of my chest of drawers, which he'd climbed up handle by handle. 'Listen,' I said to him. 'I've got to go and eat. Stay right there while I'm gone. Don't jump down and make a noise, and do not – pay attention

43

now – open anything, play with anything, *do* anything. 'Kay?'

He stopped walking about. 'You're going to eat?' he asked.

'Yeah, but don't worry about missing anything, it's not proper food, it's my mother's cooking.'

'How long will you be? I like company.'

'I'll gulp it down. Now do *nothing*, OK?'

During tea Mum went on and on for the benefit of Dad's ears about the state she'd found the kitchen in. All he did was nod and go 'Oh?' and 'Mm' every so often because he'd already heard as much as he needed to about it.

'Can I go now?' I said, once I'd thrown as much as I could take of whatever it was down my neck.

'Where?' she asked.

'Eejit's.'

'What about your room?'

'Been there. Now I'm going to Eejit's.'

'I mean have you tidied it?'

'Yes.'

'Well, I think I'll check on that, if you don't mind.'

'What if I said I did mind?'

She stood up – 'I'd still check' – and headed for the stairs.

I went after her and shoved past her on the stairs, needing to get there first and hide the bogey man. I made it ahead of her, but when I opened my door I almost passed out. The bogey man sat in the middle of a heap of clothes he'd pulled off hangers in the wardrobe, grinning his knobbly head off. I rushed forward, grabbed him, and threw him out the window. He went without a sound.

'Jiggy!' Mum said, freezing in the doorway like she'd been sledgehammered between the eyeballs.

'I know, I know,' I said miserably.

'You lied to me!'

'I didn't lie.'

'You told me you'd tidied your room.'

'I did tidy it, but...'

'I'm very disappointed in you,' she said.

'OK,' I said.

'I'm grounding you for a week.'

'OK. No, wait. A *week*?'

'And if there's any backchat it'll be longer.'

'So I can't go to school?' (There had to be a bright side to this.)

'You know very well what I mean.'

No bright side. We'd been here before. Quite a few times actually. She meant I had to spend all my free time, but not school time, alone, mostly in this room. And 'grounded' didn't just mean staying in. It meant not enjoying anything. She might allow me to read a book, but no comics that I couldn't smuggle in. If the TV in my room had worked instead of being just a dead object I threw my shirts over, it would have been removed.

'NOW TIDY THIS *UP*!!!' she shrieked.

As she left me to start my dismal week in solitary, she picked up the rackety old fan. I wasn't even going to be allowed to be cool.

As she went downstairs I heard a sound at the window. A pair of greeny-brown hands were on the ledge. A greeny-brown head looked over.

'I climbed back,' the bogey man said cheerfully.

That night it was warm yet again, so I still had to leave the window open, and because my mum had nicked the fan there was nothing to drown out the snores from Eejit's tent. I must have drifted off though, because I woke around three according to the bedside clock whose alarm I never set. Eejit was still snoring up a storm, but I don't think it was that that woke me. I think it was the bogey man moving about. He was standing at the window in his hanky-nappy, looking out. Well, not standing exactly. He was too short to see out by standing. He'd hauled himself up to the ledge to look over it.

'What's so fascinating?' I whispered.

'I want to go to the nice noise,' he said.

'What nice noise?'

'Over there.'

He raised a finger and pointed to the Atkins's garden. I got out of bed and padded to the window.

'You mean the snoring?'

'Nice noise.'

'No accounting for taste, but OK, fine, off you go.'

'There's a fence,' he said.

'So?'

'It's very high.'

'The drainpipe's higher. You climbed that.'

'And I'm frightened.'

'Frightened? What of?'

47

'Of what's making the nice noise. I don't know what it is.'

'It's called an Eejit Atkins.' He looked up at me, puzzled. 'A sort of missing link between ancient cave drawings and modern humans,' I explained.

'Will you take me to it?'

'You can count on it. Tomorrow.'

'Not tomorrow. Now. I think it's where I belong.'

'And that's a fact,' I said. 'But it's somewhere between midnight and dawn and if I went out now my mother would hear. She has ears like a bat except when I want her to listen to me.'

The little man was still hanging from the ledge looking up at me. Big bogey tears were forming in his eyes.

'Please.'

I looked away. I can't stand it when people look at me tearfully, even bogey men. But there was no way I was going to give in to him on this.

'Middle of the night, can't be done, tomorrow, OK?'

SNORT.

This wasn't either of us. It was Atkins, from next door. The snort was like a big exclamation mark

48

that shouted 'What, are you *deaf* or something?'
When he heard it the little man quivered all over,
head to bogey foot, let go of the ledge, and dropped
to the floor with his hands bunched over his eyes.
Dark tears squeezed past his little fists and
splashed onto the carpet, and he began to sob.

'Quiet,' I said. 'You'll wake the Golden Oldies.'

'I can't help it,' he wailed pitifully. 'I can't
sto-o-o-op.'

I got down on my knees, to be a bit nearer his
height. 'I could try and lob you over the fence from
here if it helps,' I offered kindly.

His bottom lip shook like a fat leaf. 'Don't want
to go on my own.'

I was stuck. If he carried on like this, Mum
would hear him and run in shouting. But if I crept
downstairs with him and out the front or back
door, she was bound to hear that too. It wouldn't
have been so bad if my room was on the ground
floor. Then I could just climb out the window. But
it wasn't. So I couldn't.

Or could I? I looked over the ledge. It was much
too far to jump if I ever wanted to walk again, but
there might be one way I could get down. The same

49

way the bogey man had last night. Same way he'd come back up, twice. I firmed my jaw in true hero fashion.

'OK. You win. But if I fall and break something, I don't want you bringing me grapes or flowers in hospital – understood?'

'Understood,' he said.

I got up from my knees – 'Might as well take this as we're going that way' – and popped Eejit's little coffin into my pyjama pocket. Then I lifted the bogey man onto my back and told him to put his arms round my neck. Shuddering a little (I never thought I'd be wearing a bogey necklace!) I threw a leg over the window ledge. Then I threw another. Then I gripped the drainpipe, lowered myself very carefully, and started down with the bogey man on my back.*

Amazingly, we made it all the way to the ground without slipping or falling off. 'Good ride,' he said as we headed for the fence.

'Thanks. Remind me not to do it again any time soon.'

The fences between the back gardens on the estate are six feet high. That means Dad can look

---

* This is not something you must try at home (even without a bogey man on your back). Ed.

over them if he stands on tiptoe and I can't unless I'm on a chair. It also means I can't climb over them all that easily. Usually. Mum had left a small ladder out after doing some gardeny stuff earlier and asked Dad to take it in for her, and he hadn't. I put the ladder against the fence and climbed up it with the bogey man still on my back, wishing I'd come out in my slippers because the hard rungs hurt my soft nude feet.

It would have been handy if there'd been an identical ladder on the other side of the fence, but there wasn't, so I told my passenger to hold tight and jumped down. It was a noisier landing than I meant it to be because of the 'Oof!' I made when I hit the ground, followed by an 'Aaaargh!' when I trod on one of Eejit's brother Jolyon's lager cans.* But no one came rushing out waving a shotgun, and the dive-bombing snores from the tent on the lawn didn't even hiccup.

'Still OK?' I whispered over my shoulder.

The bogey man didn't answer, just started humming in my ear.

I set off across the grass, running low in case of sudden searchlights from the sky looking for

---

* Jolyon tosses them out of his bedroom window when they're dead.

people in pyjamas in someone else's garden with men made of bogeys on their back. Reaching the tent I lifted one of the flaps, and looked in at Eejit Atkins's backside. He was snoozing with it in the air, his face half buried in a pillow. Unfortunately, his mouth wasn't in the buried part. If I thought his snoring was loud up in my room, this close you needed atomic earplugs. I lifted the bogey man off my back and put him on the ground beside Eejit's sleeping bag.

'See that?' I said.

'What?' he asked.

I pointed at the Atkins hooter. 'That. It's where you came from.'

He seemed a bit unsure about this, and a shadow appeared at his feet and began to climb the tent wall with its hands raised like claws, its mouth open wide like it would snap the head off the first person to say 'Hey, you're a shadow of your former self.' But halfway to the peak of the tent it seemed to change its mind about being menacing and withered back to the feet it had sprung from. The bogey man looked up at me then. He was smiling.

'Home,' he said.

At that moment Eejit's back end collapsed and he turned over with a piglike snuffle. I hoped he might stop snoring on his back, but he started all over again, louder than ever. You might have thought the little man would have been worried by such a row up close, but now that he'd got used to it he couldn't seem to get enough of it. Or near enough to it. He leaned over and stroked Eejit's nose.

'Home,' he said again, and as he said it he began to shrink, like his shadow had done before him. The hanky-nappy fell off and before my very eyes he got smaller and smaller and smaller still. When Eejit gave another of his super-snorts the bogey man jumped and stopped shrinking. But then he smiled again and climbed onto the nearest Atkins shoulder, gazed adoringly up his snout, and shrank some more. When he was down to the size he was when I first saw him, he gripped the rim of a nostril with both hands and began hauling himself into it, head first. Up he went into Eejit's nose, up and up and up, until all that was left of him were his itsy little feet, twitching goodbye.

Then he was gone. Back where he belonged,

53

with all the other bogeys that lurk in Eejit Atkins's snotty head.

Eejit's brain being what it was – a very small bowl of mashed swede – he'd probably forgotten by now that he'd ever made the little coffin, but I left it on his pillow anyway before heading back. Again I ran low in case of searchlights, but I managed to avoid stray lager cans this time. Climbing back over the fence wasn't easy because of the ladder famine on the Atkins side, but I made it. I also made it up the drainpipe, though for the first time ever I wished I'd put in more effort all the times Mr Rice had ordered me up ropes in the gym.

Because I'd been up half of yet another night, I was moving even slower than usual next morning. If it had been Saturday I could have spent extra time in bed, but it wasn't, so I had to get up for school, curse it. Pete and Angie had gone on without me again, and who should I bump into the other side of my gate but Eejit, holding a hand over his nose. He mumbled something into the hand when he saw me.

'Sorry?' I said.

He gave a horrible sniff. 'I godd a goldd,' he mumbled.

'Serve you right, sleeping out of doors night after night and keeping me awake.'

'S'all loose in me 'ead,' he explained.

'What, yer brain?'

'The moocus. I woulda stayed 'ome agin, but me mum said no, cos she faand aat I skived orf yesterdy and she weren't 'appy abaat...' He didn't finish because he felt a sneeze coming on. 'Ah-ah-ah-aaaah...'

As he screwed his eyes up and tilted his head back I had a flash vision of everything in his manky skull shooting out, all over the pavement, parked cars, me, and joining up into a hundred little bogey men, all keen to turn my world upside down and make my life even more complicated than it already was.

'Atkins!' I yelled. 'Don't you dare!'

Snatching the latest neatly folded hanky from my pocket and wrapping it round his nose, I squeezed it to stop anything escaping and threw my other arm round his neck so he couldn't jerk away.

'McCue! What did I tell you about bullying?!'

Mr Rice, tutor of my least-favourite lesson, jogging to school.

'It's not what it looks like,' I said, still holding Eejit in a crucifying armlock and hankying his conk.

'Looks enough like it to me!' the Ricicle bawled. 'Let go of that boy and see me after school!'

I let Atkins go and Mr R jogged on.

'Terrific,' I sighed, watching him go. 'An after-school talking-to in an especially deep voice from Tracksuit Man.'

My efforts to stop the Big Sneeze had worked, though. There was a small implosion in Eejit's head, the sneeze stayed inside, and I threw my hanky into a passing wastebin, panic over.

But then I noticed something dangling from Eejit's nose. Hanging down across his mouth, all the way to his chin.

The little bogey man.

The sneeze must have knocked him loose, maybe woken him up and kicked him out of his bogey bed. He hung from one of his master's nostrils like a mountaineer who's missed his footing. I've heard of cliffhanger endings, but this was ridiculous. A *nose*-hanger?

The bogey man grinned when he saw me, and gave a cheery wave. Atkins noticed me gawping at his schnoz.

'Wossup?'

'Something on your nose,' I said.

'Yeah?'

And he wiped his arm across it.

'Is it gorn?'

'Er...yes.'

I looked at his sleeve. There was a greeny-brown smear on it.

A greeny-brown smear that wasn't moving.

Or grinning.

And certainly not waving cheerily.

Jiggy McCue

GRANDPA'S EXTRA HOLE

by
Pete Garrett

I dont talk about stuff tht happenes to me like Jiggy does. But there was this one thinge, and when i told him about it he said i had to rite it down. writtings not my thing, i said to him and he said right it anyway an i'll correctt the speling, punchuate it propply and make sence of your roten sentances. That mans a control freak. I kept saying i wasnt gonna do it but he went on an on so in the end i scribbled it down anywy, t get him off my back. This bit hears the only bit I wouldnt let him touch. Anyway heres the story what I wrote! (yeah, I know what I wrote is wrong. Its delibarate, to anoy mcCue wen he reeds it)

My grandpa had an extra hole. No, don't laugh. How would you like it? Doesn't a person have enough holes without extras? It's a wonder the rain doesn't get in as it is.

It wouldn't have been so bad if Grandpa's extra hole had been some sort of use. But it wasn't. He couldn't see with it, hear with it, eat with it, sniff with it, blow through it, even make noises with it. OK, you ask, so where was it, this useless extra hole? You'll never guess, so I'd better tell you. It was in the back of his neck − the base of his skull really, but he got a kick out of saying it was the back of his neck. 'Gives a "hole" new meaning to talking out of the back of your neck,' he would say.

You couldn't see the hole. Hair covered it. Gramps didn't have much hair up above, so it was like it had all slid down from the top. This bundle of grey hair, like an old horse's tail, jutted out over his collar, bound together with an elastic band. A yellow one. Always yellow. My dad says Grandpa used to be a hippy and still thought of himself as one even though he's collecting his pension and could get meals-on-wheels if he wanted.

Once, just once, Grandpa gave me a guided tour of the back of his head. He parted the horse's tail and asked if I could see the extra hole. You couldn't miss it. It looked like someone had dipped a teaspoon in the bottom of his skull and scooped out what was there.

'Stick your finger in,' he said.

'Hey, don't know about that,' I said.

'Go on, it won't bite.'

I took a deep breath and stuck my finger in the extra hole. It didn't bite.

'Now press,' he said.

'Grandpa…'

'Go on, Petey. Press.'

He always called me Petey. Had since I was little. No one else ever did, and that was fine with me.

I pressed a finger against the back of the hole. Nothing happened.

'Nothing happened,' I said.

'What did you expect?' Grandpa answered. 'My skull to spring open like a cuckoo clock? Give it a tap.'

'A tap?'

'With the end of your finger.'

I tapped. With my finger end. There was a hollow sort of clang.

'What's that?' I asked.

Was my grandfather some sort of android and nobody'd bothered to tell me? If so, what did that make me? Or my dad, come to that?

'That's my plate,' he said. 'I got it in the war. Almost bought it.'

'You almost bought a plate for your head in the war?'

'I mean I almost died. There was this terrible explosion. Shrapnel everywhere. You know what shrapnel is?'

'Well,' I said.

'It's what they put in shells. Bits of metal and bullets and things, so when the shell explodes the stuff goes flying all over the place and more people get hurt.'

'And you got hit by this...?'

'Shrapnel. Yeah. Right there in the back of my skull. Nearly did for me. But there was this temporary field hospital nearby, and they were able to dig it out and put a metal plate in my skull to hold the shattered bone together.'

'Not a dinner plate then,' I said. 'Doesn't have "Made-in-Wherever" on the back.'

Grandpa chuckled. He liked a good joke, Grandpa. Dad always said that was where I got my jokiness. From Grandpa.

'The trouble with having a plate like that in your head,' said Gramps the day he showed me his extra hole, 'is that you have to watch what you go near.'

'Why?' I asked.

'It's magnetic. Other nearby metal things fly to it and stick to it. When your gran was alive I didn't dare go too near her sewing basket. The one time I did, it took her ages to pull the pins out of my neck. I was in agony.'

He grinned that long-toothed yellow grin of his. Whenever he grinned that grin I wondered if I'd just heard a porky or if he'd told me a true story. Impossible to tell with my grandpa. But it didn't matter. I didn't care. His stories were always worth hearing.

I mentioned the shrapnel to Dad once, not long after I heard about it. Dad laughed. 'Shrapnel!' he said. 'War!'

'What do you mean?'

'What war do you think he was in, Pete?'

I didn't know. There've been a lot of wars and

Gramps was pretty ancient, so it could have been any one of them.

'The only war my dad was ever in was the war of the sexes,' Dad told me. 'The enemy was your grandma, the whole time I was growing up.'

'Gramps and Grandma used to fight?' I said.

'Like ferrets.'

'So…what? Gran gave him the extra hole?'

Dad chuckled. 'It wasn't your gran. Wasn't anyone really. He got it on a building site.'

'Building site!'

'He used to be a bricky. You knew that, didn't you?'

'Yes…'

Fact was that I'd heard so many of Grandpa's stories about his life that I wasn't sure what was actually what.

'One day, way back,' my dad said, 'he and some workmates were chucking stuff about while the foreman was away, and Dad fell off some scaffolding and these bits of metal got lodged in the back of his head. He was whisked off to hospital and operated on, but they decided it was safer to leave the last bit in. Better in than out, they said, and it's been there ever since.' He laughed. 'Shrapnel!'

I was disappointed with the real story, but not too much. The hole still existed after all, and how many grandfathers are there with holes in their skulls that don't contain eyeballs, wax, snot or bacon baps? That made him pretty unusual. I liked having an unusual grandpa. I never told Gramps that I knew the truth. The hole truth, you might say. I didn't want him to know I knew. If he'd turned the accidental hole into a story to entertain me that was fine with me. I appreciated it.

Grandpa and his stories. When I was little and he and Gran visited, or we visited them, he would sit on a chair beside my bed at bedtime and tell me them, one after the other. Reel them off, he would, straight out of his head. His stories were about all sorts of things – dragons and monsters, aliens, adventurers – but the ones I liked best were about him when he was young, him and his pals and the things they got up to. I liked to hear about living in the city, like he did then, and his school life, and his parents, who I never knew, and his travels when he was old enough to go off on his own, and his girlfriends. Grandpa's face really lit up when he talked about his old girlfriends. It made me laugh, hearing about them. My grandpa chasing girls! Girls chasing him! I loved Grandpa's stories.

He used to visit quite often when we lived on Borderline Way, before Mum walked out and Gran got run over by the bus for the blind, and sometimes we would go to stay with him in the West Country. We stopped seeing so much of him after we moved to the Brook Farm Estate with Angie and her mum. We had a spare room at Borderline Way, but there are four of us here and we use all three bedrooms. He could have had my bed. I wrote and told him that. 'I'll sleep on the couch if you come to stay,' I said. But he didn't come. He said new houses made him nervous, but I think that was just an excuse. The only time he came here was one half-term when Angie and her mum were away on one of their girlie holidays.

That's the time I want to write about.

It was the evening before Ange and Aud went, and I was in my room, at my PC, thinking of kicking the thing to rubble because it was on a go-slow. When you zap the enemy you want to trash them right away, you don't want to give them time to duck. Duck? They didn't have the energy even for that.

When Dad came in he noticed that I was the fastest thing in the room even though I was sitting still, and he looked over my shoulder. Dad knows about computers. It's his business, building them, fixing them, upgrading them. He built mine out of spare parts, and usually it was pretty smooth, but it'd been getting slower and slower for weeks. I'd been meaning to mention it, but you know how it is. He told me to shift while he took a look-see.

'It's all these games you've downloaded,' he said. 'They're clogging up the memory. You'll have to bin some.'

'I can't,' I said. 'I need them. All of them.'

He thought about this, then said, 'As it happens you could be in luck. A pair of Malaysian memory chips arrived the other day for me to try out. Revolutionary, they claim. I've installed one in my desktop to give it a run. Packs quite a kick. I'll pop the other one in yours if you like...'

'Yes please,' I said.

The chip was tiny, sort of like a watch battery to look at. How any kind of memory could be housed in something that small was a mystery. But when Dad fitted it and I launched one of my war games, the two armies shook their heads, squared their shoulders, and started wiping one another out so fast it was hard to keep up with them.

'Impressive,' Dad said.

'Impressive? It's incredible!'

'Got something to show off to your grandpa now.'

'Grandpa?' I said, still watching the double massacre.

'He's coming the day after tomorrow.'

I looked at him. 'He's coming here? To stay?'

'Just while Aud and Angie are away.'

'Why am I always the last to know stuff?' I said.

'You're not,' he said. 'I haven't told Aud yet.'

He went downstairs and told her right away, and I heard her reply. Hard not to. She'd only met Gramps twice and she said he was a dirty old man. Dirty fingernails and grubby clothes, she meant. I heard Dad say that that's why he was coming while she was away, so she wouldn't be able to turn her nose up at him.

Angie came into my room a minute later. She knew the way I felt about Grandpa.

'She didn't mean it,' she said.

'Who didn't mean what?' I said, zapping like crazy.

'Mum. About your grandpa.'

'Dunno what you mean.' Zapp-zapp.

'OK.'

She went out. Closed the door after her.

When Dad picked Grandpa up from the station two days later and brought him home I thought he didn't look so good. I told him so. 'Hay-fever season,' he said.

'Since when did you get hay fever?' I asked.

'Every spring,' he said.

'I never knew.'

'You probably never saw me in the spring before.'

I knew hay fever. Audrey got it pretty bad – sniffles, runny nose, red eyes – and Angie did too, in small doses. Grandpa just looked kind of weak, and kept trailing off in the middle of sentences and looking kind of lost. That wasn't like any hay fever I knew.

71

'It's not hay fever,' Dad said when we were alone. 'It's old age.'

Old. Yeah. Gramps was my oldest relative not counting the dead ones. He became a dad for the first time when he was forty-two. His first child was my Auntie Wendy, who moved to New Zealand when I was five or six. My father came into the world two years after her, which made Gramps eighty-four now because Dad had just turned forty. Eighty-four. Maybe he was entitled to feel a little weak and forget what he was saying occasionally.

The day after he arrived we went into town on the bus. Just Gramps and me, Dad was at work. It's not far to town, and usually I walk, or bike it, but Dad said the walk would be a strain for Gramps and he gave me the return bus fare (Gramps had a bus pass) and enough for two snacks at the Italian Café in Mussolini Arcade.

The Italian Café was a place Gramps mentioned in letters all the time. He once had a good bit of cake there, and he liked the coffee, and he said the chick behind the counter was a dead-ringer for young Sophie Loran or someone. He even knew the chick's name – Daniela – and he was really disappointed she was nowhere to be seen when we got there.

'Probably her day off,' I said. 'We'll come again another day. She's bound to be here another day.'

'You're a good lad, Petey,' he said.

'Regular saint,' I said.

He laughed at that. 'Regular saint,' he repeated, and for a mo he was his old self. But then a sort of fog passed over his eyes.

'You all right?' I asked him.

He looked at me blankly for a bit, then shook his shoulders, and the fog cleared. 'My mind's going, Petey. Some days I look in the mirror and think "Who the devil's that old twit?" Old age, it stinks, son, and don't let anyone tell you otherwise. Count yourself lucky age is on your side. Sure ain't on mine. See these legs? They're my last. On my last legs, geddit?'

He laughed at this too. Gramps was a great laugher at himself. When he laughed about being on his last legs I wished that I could reach over and hug him. Say something like, 'Legs, shmegs, you've always got me, Gramps.' But we Garretts don't do wet stuff like hugs. Even my mum didn't do that much.

73

When we finished our elevenses, we walked slowly to the door of the café. I never walked so slowly in my life. I opened the door for him, and he tottered out and almost went flying as four cement-brains elbowed him out of the way.

'You wanna put the old fart back in his Zimmer, Garrett,' Jolyon Atkins said as I caught Grandpa's bony elbow to stop him falling.

'You wanna get back in your cage, Atkins,' I said. 'Must be coming up to feeding time.'

'Watch it, sunshine,' Jolyon snarled, glaring down at me.

'Watch it yourself,' I snarled, glaring up at him.

I expected him to grab me by the shirt and hoick me to eye level, maybe butt my head while I was there, but he just snarled another threat and he and his pulphead pals dragged themselves off along the pavement.

We found a bench by the shopping centre flower beds, which were nearby. When we were settled I asked him how he was doing. He winked at me.

'Hunky-dory, boy. Hunky-dory.'

He took a little box out of his jacket pocket.

'What's that?'

'Pills to keep me going. Should have taken one first thing. Forgot.'

I looked at the label. I couldn't even think about pronouncing the name of the pills, but I liked the instruction printed underneath. *Take one capsule twice a day.*

'The same capsule twice a day?' I said. 'Isn't it a bit messy the second time?'

He thought that was very funny. I was glad he hadn't forgotten how to laugh yet.

He took a small flask from another pocket and tipped it to his mouth to swallow the capsule.

'Medicinal?' I said.

'No, just booze,' he replied.

After that he leaned back and watched the people moving around the square, going into the shops, coming out, standing together, talking. He looked kind of down, and I didn't know what to say to him. I don't think this ever happened before. We never had any shortage of talkie stuff, Grandpa and me, mostly because he was such a great natterer. It felt like sitting with a stranger. Maybe it was just me, though, because in a while he said, 'Nice, isn't it?'

'What is?'

'You and me, sitting here, watching the people go by, smelling the…what are they called?'

He meant the flowers. 'Washing machines,' I said.

A big yellow grin sliced his face in two.

'Washing machines! You'll be the death of me, Ollie.'

My expression must have changed when he said that, because his grin died and he came over all concerned.

'What?' he said. 'Did I say something?'

He'd called me Ollie. He'd called me by my dad's name. His son's. For a second, Pete Garrett, his grandson, had stopped existing.

'No,' I said.

We headed for the bus stop shortly after that. Didn't say much on the way. On the bus, I caught him rubbing the back of his head.

'What is it?' I asked.

'The shrapnel,' he replied. 'Always itches in the autumn.'

'It's spring, Gramps.'

'Didn't I say that?'

'Yeah. Course you did.'

But he knew he hadn't. 'I'm a mess, Petey,' he

76

said. I was glad he got my name right this time. 'It's what you get for living this long. Sort of an anti-reward. Take my advice, son, don't ever get old.'

'No chance,' I said. 'I'm giving old-age the thumbs down.'

He smirked. 'Staying young forever, are you?'

'Too right.'

'You think so now, but one day if you're lucky – lucky! – you'll be sitting here, or somewhere, talking to a kid of your own, or a grandkid, and you'll be grey or bald, probably both, with bags under your eyes, a walk like a wounded spider, and this kid will be saying how he's never going to do something as uncool as get old. It's the way things work. The way they come around.'

In the next couple of days I didn't spend as much time with Grandpa as I expected to before he came. I didn't want to. He wasn't such great company any more, and he looked like someone falling apart inside a straitjacket. One yank of the Velcro and his insides would burst out and dribble down the wallpaper.

I played games on my super-fast PC a lot of the time. The revolutionary Malaysian memory chip was a blast. But my mind kept returning to Grandpa sitting downstairs watching daytime TV like a billion other oldies, and I felt so...you know...sad. My grandpa, my lively, story-telling grandpa, was suddenly just another old person, his life so far behind him that it was like it happened to someone else.

Jiggy called for me a couple of times. We went to the Councillor Snit Memorial Park once, sat on the swings, kicked litter about, and another time we went to his house and talked about nothing much. When I went out and did these things I felt bad about not being with Grandpa. Dad was out at work during the day, so it was just me and Gramps, and I'd abandoned him to daytime TV hell.

It was on the fifth morning of Grandpa's visit that the Big Thing happened. He'd been dozing in front of the box and I was sitting nearby for a change, looking through the comic that had just arrived, and he suddenly snapped awake and asked if there was a snooker hall about.

'Snooker hall?' I said. 'You want to watch snooker?'

'Watch it? No, I don't want to watch it, I want to *play* it!'

This was a surprise. All the time I'd known him, which was all my life, he'd never mentioned snooker. I had no idea it interested him.

'There's a snooker hall above Fit Types,' I said.

'Fit Types?'

'The keep-fit zoo. Me, Jig and Ange go there sometimes.'

'What for? You don't need to keep fit at your age.'

'I mean upstairs, the snooker hall. We play pool usually.'

'Any good?' he asked.

'It's OK.'

'I mean you.'

'Oh yeah. Genius level.'

'You'll have to be,' said Grandpa. 'I used to be a killer at snooker when I was a lad.'

'Not for a while then.'

'You don't forget these things. It's like falling off a bike. Come on, Ollie, my treat.'

Ollie again. But I didn't pick him up on it. At least he wanted to do something.

When we left the house I saw something amazing

over the road. Jiggy hanging with Eejit Atkins, Jolyon's moron kid brother. Eejit's Jig's next-door neighbour. He was skateboarding up walls and lampposts and Jig was watching him. Must be desperate, I thought. He probably was. Angie was away, I was spending most of my time indoors, and there weren't many other kids we knew on the estate.

Jig spotted us. 'Hey!' he yelled.

'Hey,' I yelled back. Half yelled. I didn't feel much like yelling after being called Ollie again.

Jig hopped across the road. 'Hi, Grandpa!' (Him and Ange have always called him Grandpa.) 'Whereya going?' he asked.

'Town,' I said.

'Can I come?'

'No.'

He leaned closer. 'Pete. I'm watching Eejit Atkins *skateboard*!'

'Well enjoy yourself,' I said, grabbing Grandpa's elbow and walking him away. McCue had a mother and father, two grandparents and a cat. I only had a father and grandfather and I didn't want to share Grandpa now he was on those last legs of his.

'Aren't you embarrassed, being seen with an old

'fossil like me?' Gramps asked as we walked.

'Are you kidding?' I said. 'I collect fossils.'

That tickled him. It was good to hear him laugh again.

At the end of the road we waited for the bus. While we waited he leant against the bus stop post, like he would fall down if he didn't. He didn't look too great, but whenever he caught me looking he made an effort to brighten up. He didn't want me to see him old and senile, which is probably why he'd suggested snooker. He wanted us to be like we used to be. Grandpa and Grandson. It was taking a lot out of him, I could tell, but I played along.

Fit Types shares a street door with the snooker hall upstairs. Most times you have to stand back and let wads of big red-faced women out before you can get in, but today it was a skinny little man in a green tracksuit, who looked about as much of a Fit Type as Grandpa.

'It'll kill me in the end, all this exercise,' he said, and tottered off with one hand on the wall.

We started up the stairs. Gramps was wheezing by stair five. I called a halt at stair eight to let him get some breath back.

'Taken your pill for the first time today?' I asked him.

He said he had and was looking forward to taking it again later.

There were only four tables in the snooker hall. Teenage boys were on a couple of them and the two serious men on the third looked like they should be wearing waistcoats and bending over for the TV cameras. Grandpa went straight to the fourth table and grabbed a cue. He didn't look strong enough to grip it, let alone do anything with it, so I suggested that we just watch the others for a while.

'Why?' he said. 'Afraid I'll whip you?'

'No, I just thought…'

'We came here to play, and play we will. Let's go!'

'OK,' I said, and made like I was about to head for the door.

He chuckled. 'Get back here, lad, and prepare to be defeated!'

I smirked. 'You don't stand a chance. I'll massacre you.'

'We'll see about that,' said Gramps. 'Grab your bat.'

'They're called cues.'

'I knew that. Grab one.'

I grabbed a cue. 'Who's going to break?'

'Me, probably,' he said.

'I mean who goes first?'

'After you, Ollie.'

This went right through me, sharp as a snooker cue. And this time I didn't let it go.

'Grandpa,' I said. 'Do you know who I am?'

He flashed his yellow choppers. 'What a question. Course I know who you are, I only have one grandson.'

OK, I thought. Long as he remembers that, what does a name matter?

I chalked my cue and slammed the white ball into the reds, which scattered in all directions. One of them shot into a pocket, then shot out again.

'What do you get for that?' Grandpa asked.

'Two million points,' I said. 'Your turn.'

'What do I do?'

'I thought you knew about snooker.'

'I do. Just can't remember which ball to hit.'

'Cue the white. Try and pot a red. Any red.'

'No problem.'

He found the white ball, leaned over his cue, brought his bony elbow back, and...

...fell face down on the green baize.

At the hospital, Dad said: 'Don't let it get you down, Pete. These things happen.'

'Oh yeah, sure. Like every day I kill my grandfather.'

'You didn't kill him. He's not dead.'

'Not far off it.'

'If it's anyone's fault it's mine,' said Dad. 'I should never have let him come all this way. I had no idea he was so poorly.'

We sat on opposite sides of the bed, looking at Grandpa with all these tubes and wires attached to him. He was spark out, snoring so quietly you could hardly hear him.

'We were never very close,' Dad said after a while.

'You weren't?'

I thought how close Gramps and I had always been. I couldn't imagine not being close to Gramps.

'He never told me stories, like he did my sister and you.'

'No?'

'Just once or twice when I was small.'

He looked really down in the dumps. 'He talks about you all the time,' I said, hoping it would help.

It seemed to. He looked across the bed at me, eyes so wide you'd think they'd been stitched open.

'He does?'

'Yeah. You'd be amazed how often your name comes up.'

There was a small dry chuckle. Grandpa was awake. And looking at me.

'Hi, Wendy,' he said.

His fingers twitched. They were trying to reach my hand. Or his daughter's. I moved mine closer. His thin old fingers fell on top of it.

'How's life in Auckland?'

'Auckland?'

'Still thinks you're Wendy,' Dad whispered.

'Oh, Auckland,' I said. 'Yes, it's…great.'

He just sat there after that, looking at the daughter I wasn't, with this huge watery-eyed love. I sat it out, but deep inside I felt kind of hurt. My grandpa, my own grandpa on those

85

last legs of his, not knowing me.

But then he turned his gaze on Dad. 'Did you bring the catapult, Sid?'

Dad looked at me and I looked at him. Both of us were thinking '*Who*?' Sid could've been someone Grandpa knocked about with when he was my age, or he could have been no one at all. A figment. I looked back at Grandpa. His memory was almost gone. The bits of it that counted anyway.

But then an idea came to me.

A really wild idea.

Back home in my PC there was this fantastically powerful memory chip. If the miracle Malaysian chip could give a computer the kind of bounce it had given mine, maybe it could juice up a human's memory. Grandpa's. And if it improved his memory maybe it would also give him a new lease of life physically too.

It was worth a try.

'Dad, can I come back?'

'Back?'

'In half an hour or so. I just remembered something I have to do at home.'

'Well...'

He looked suddenly lonely. But I had to go. I jumped up and left him. I didn't say goodbye to Grandpa because – well, I didn't want to say goodbye to him.

I wished I'd brought my bike, because it's quite a scoot from the hospital to the estate. Took me about fifteen minutes on foot, which was about fourteen more than my legs can take without starting to wobble. Having a stitch most of the way didn't help. At home I gasped my way up to my room, whipped the chip out of my PC, and bumped down again on my backside. Then I headed back to the hospital – on my bike. Six minutes max. There was nowhere near the entrance to chain my bike and I didn't want to waste time looking for a rack, so I just dropped it.

'Hey! Kid! You can't leave your bike there!' a security-type uniform yelled.

'I know!' I said. 'Watch it for me, willya!'

I ducked under his arm, ran through the swivel doors to the lobby, and up the stairs to the ward. Grandpa was asleep again. Dad hadn't moved.

'Looks like you could do with a break,' I said when I'd got some of my breath back. 'There's a caff on the ground floor.'

87

He glanced at his own dad. 'I'd better stay. Just in case.'

'Oh, he'll be all right for a minute,' I said. 'Go on, Dad. Go. Go.'

He hesitated, but then he got up. 'Glad you're here, Pete,' he said.

'Yeah. Glad you're here too.'

I waited till all the nurses were in the office at the far end, then nudged the curtain round just enough to stop anyone seeing us if they looked our way. There was only one person who could see us now – another oldie, across the aisle in another bed – but he was either in a really heavy sleep or a coma, so I wasn't too bothered about him.

'Grandpa,' I whispered.

'Zzzzzzzzzzzzzzzzz.'

'I want to try something, Gramps. It won't hurt. Probably won't work. But I want to try it anyway and I hope you won't consider it a liberty or an invasion of your personal space or anything.'

'Zzzzzzzzzzzzzzzzz.'

I didn't like to move him in case one of the wires or tubes popped out and alarms went off and thousands of hospital people came running with trolleys loaded with equipment and started thumping his chest. But I had to. I pulled his head gently forward and felt under his horse's mane for the extra hole at the base of his skull, and slipped the revolutionary Malaysian memory chip in. When it was about halfway in, it sort of tugged away from me, and there was this tiny little clang. The chip had been drawn to the metal plate that wasn't shrapnel but something from a building site.

I laid Grandpa's head carefully back on the pillow and sat down to see if anything happened. I was still sitting there, still waiting, when Dad came back.

'No change?' he said.

Grandpa was still snoring softly. 'No.'

He sat down on the other side of the bed, like before. 'You know he's probably not going to get any better, Pete.' It wasn't a question.

'I know.' But I had to give it a go, I said to myself.

But then I had another thought. Not a good one. I saw how what I'd done would look to others. Like something really desperate. Something pretty damn stupid. You're a klutz, Garrett, I thought

89

next. Only an absolute dumb-head would seriously think that shoving a computer memory chip into a living, breathing person's extra hole would—

'Hi, Petey. How ya doin', pal?'

A hand clapped onto mine. An old dry hand. Grandpa's.

I looked at his face. There was colour in his cheeks, and his lips were twitching in a real Grampsy smile. Maybe I wasn't such a klutz or dumbo after all.

Dad couldn't believe it. Unlike me he hadn't had any reason to hope this might happen. The doctors had told him that his father was shuffling towards the exit, and here he was, all chirpy and bright-eyed again.

'How's it going, Ollie?'

As he said this he took Dad's hand too. I'd never seen that before. My father and grandfather holding hands. But it was nice. I was happy to see it.

'You look so…well,' my father said.

'Never felt better,' said Gramps, and he winked at me, like he knew what I'd done. 'Want a story, Petey?' He didn't seem to notice the cables and wires and things running in and out of him, or being in a hospital bed. He just carried on as if we were at home, or on a bench in the park or somewhere.

'You bet,' I said.

'Well, let's see, what shall we...Oh, I've got one. Ready?'

'Yes, Gramps.'

He grinned at me, then he grinned at Dad, and he kept hold of our hands as he said: 'It's about something that happened when I was a youngster... about your age...'

And when he said 'about your age' he looked just as much at Dad as he did at me. Dad seemed very pleased.

The story Grandpa told us was about a time he and his two best mates got into this old dark spooky house that was up for demolition, and how they'd been absolutely certain they weren't alone. It was a haunted house story, and it was a wonder he hadn't told it before if it was true, but I didn't mind if it was true or made up. All I cared about was that my old grandpa was himself again, smiling and cheerful, and telling stories. But best of all, he knew me, he recognised me, he could tell me apart from his son and his daughter once

91

more. That was definitely the best bit.

When a nurse came by and saw that Grandpa had made this miraculous recovery she just gaped. Then she called a doctor, who came with some other nurses, and they just stared and stared at old Gramps.

'What are you lot gawking at?' he said to them. 'Never seen a geriatric before?' Then he yawned. He looked so contented. Really happy about that story, which he'd just finished before the nurse arrived. Pleased about Dad and me being there too.

'It would be best if he got some sleep now,' the doc said.

'He's going to be all right, isn't he?' I said.

'Let's just wait and see, shall we?'

Grandpa's eyes were closed by this time and he was snoring quietly again, but he still looked really well, and there was a little smile on his lips. I patted his hand.

'See ya, Gramps,' I whispered.

Back home, Dad and I had a drink to celebrate. He had a beer, I had a SmartSave Ultra Fizz. Later, he came to my room.

'I just took a look at my PC,' he said. 'The

revolutionary Malaysian memory chip seems to have expired.'

'Expired?'

'Packed up. So much for that. Just as well I didn't order a bundle of them before running a full test. How's yours doing?'

I kick-started my favourite war game. The two armies were back to the way they were before Dad put the chip in. Useless. I couldn't tell him that it was because the chip wasn't there any more.

'Well, you have to try these things,' he said.

'Yes,' I said. 'You have to try.'

It was about four in the morning when the phone rang. I didn't answer it, and neither did Dad at first. I felt a great weight on my chest. The only people who phone at four in the morning without good reason are pranksters and idiots.

Unless it's bad news.

Then I heard Dad talking quietly. I couldn't hear what he said but I knew from his tone of voice that it wasn't a hoax call. Then I heard him outside my door.

It opened. He looked in.

'Pete,' he called softly.

'Awake,' I said.

He came further in. Stopped about halfway between my bed and the door.

'It's your grandpa.'

'Thought it might be.'

He paused. 'It was very peaceful,' he said at last.

'Good.'

'They said he was smiling.'

'Good.'

'And he said something just before he went.'

'What did he say?'

'He said…'

I sat up. 'What did he say, Dad?'

'He said…"Good boy".'

'Are you sure it wasn't goodbye?' I asked.

'That's what I said. They said no, it was definitely "Good boy".'

'Hey,' I said.

'Yeah,' said Dad.

We smiled at one another in the half dark.

Two good boys together.

Pete Garrett

TWINKLYSTINK

by
Angie Mint

My name's Angie. Angie Mint. I live on the Brook Farm Estate with my mum and Pete Garrett and Pete's dad Oliver. We have our ups and downs, the four of us. It's not always easy sharing roofs and bathrooms with people who aren't all family — specially when one of them's Pete — but we rub along well enough most of the time. Still, every now and then Mum and I take off on our own for a bit, and this is what we did for a couple of weeks in August about a year ago, when I was twelve. We went to stay with Doug and Debra Dobro at their house, Ditherer's Dump. Debra's my mum's sister, which of course makes her my auntie, and Doug is Deb's husband. They don't have any kids, but they have a dog called Dick, so I guess you could call them 'D' people. It would be quite cool if they rounded this off by being doctors or dentists or drain detectives, but they didn't. I'll come to what they did for a living in a minute.

Dick the dog was some sort of crossbreed. Ragged-haired, smaller than most dogs, skinny little legs. He was also the most miserable mutt you ever saw, of any size or breed. He shuffled along with his head down all the time, dragging his paws, never wagging his tail or jumping up at you. He didn't even bark when the postman came. Auntie Deb washed and blow-dried him every week so he looked all clean and fluffy, but little Dick still seemed unhappy. Eventually they took him to a vet to find out what was wrong with him (Dick, not the vet). Debra told Mum and me how the consultation went, starting with the vet saying that he'd seen this sort of thing before, in other canines, and that he suspected that Dick was depressed about being a dog.

'Why would he be depressed about being a dog?' Doug asked. 'What else could he be?'

'Well,' the vet said, 'if his atoms had been differently assembled he could be a pig, a cow or a ruined cottage in Majorca. But he's not any of those things. He's a dog, and he doesn't appreciate it. Do you believe in reincarnation?'

'No,' said Doug.

'If he's reincarnated, he could have been a pigeon last time. Imagine. Flying wherever he wanted, dropping messages on any head he chose. If he was previously a pigeon, you can see why four legs and no wings might get him down, can't you? Quite a drop in freedom, only going out on a leash, and always on the ground.'

'Can you do anything for him?' Debra asked.

'I could put him to sleep,' said the vet. 'That should cure him.'

'To sleep? You mean kill him?'

'We prefer to say "put to sleep".'

'Excuse me,' said Doug, a bit narked, 'but are you...*qualified*?'

The vet pointed at the wall. 'There's the certificate.'

Deb and Doug looked at the wall. 'There's nothing there,' said Deb.

The vet laughed. 'Oh, I forgot. It's away being repaired.'

'Why would a certificate have to be repaired?'

'Not the certificate, the glass. A customer threw his dog's bone at it.'

'I'm not surprised,' said Doug. 'Let's go Deb. Dick.'

Back home, they put Dick on a course of doggy vitamins from the pharmacy, but Dick remained as droopy-eared and down-in-the-mouth as ever, so they decided to just put up with it and hope he didn't get out on his own and throw himself under a train to cheer himself up.

When Mum and I went to stay with Debra and Doug that time, they showed us round their farm, which we hadn't seen before. The tour didn't take long because it wasn't a huge farm like most. The reason it wasn't as big as others was that their one and only crop was bonsai trees, which as you probably know aren't much higher than a three-year-old's kneecap as a rule. The hundreds of trees they'd grown took up about as much space as the average classroom.

Before they became bonsai farmers, Deb and Doug did very different kinds of work. She was an art teacher and he was a research chemist. They might still have been in those jobs if the government hadn't decided to close half the nation's art departments and Doug's firm hadn't folded following a scandal about dodgy drug trials in Africa. They were actually waiting their turn in the dole queue when they hit on a new line of work. Deb was looking at a bonsai tree on the dole office window ledge.

'Bonsais are so cute,' she said. 'But I can't really see the point of them.'

'Me neither,' said Doug. 'I'd appreciate them more if they were a bit bigger. Not actual tree size, just two or three times bigger. If they were three times bigger they would look quite neat on patios, round fishponds and the like.'

'Could they be grown bigger?' Deb asked.

'Sure. Just don't cut them back so often.'

'Take ages for them to get to a reasonable size from scratch, though, wouldn't it?'

'Not if you know how to tweak their genetic code to speed their growth, it wouldn't.'

'Do you?'

'Sure.'

'So why don't we give it a go?'

'What for?'

'To see if we can make a living out of it.'

For a quarter of a minute or so, Doug just stared at her. But then he said: 'Mm, why not?'

And that's what they did. They got a Small

...iness Loan to get started, bought a stock of little bonsais, Doug tweaked their genetic codes, and in a couple of months they'd grown up to his waist. But then they hit a problem. The problem was that there wasn't much call for tall bonsai trees. People liked them small. That was their charm, apparently. After months of failing to interest buyers, Deb and Doug chopped the whole lot up, stacked the wood in the cellar, and started over, this time going the traditional route, small and slow. To bring in a little cash while the non-genetically-engineered trees grew from nothing to not much more, Debra made clothes-pegs out of the unwanted bonsai timber in the cellar, put on a shawl, and stood on street corners trying to sell them to people who felt sorry for her. Her pegs weren't standard pegs, though. Because she was an artist, she carved patterns into them and painted them. They looked terrific, but she didn't make enough out of them to do more than pay the weekly food bill.

By the time Mum and I went to stay with them for that fortnight, they were doing reasonably well with the actual size bonsais without getting rich off them. Their house was quite old. My room was right up under the eaves with a sloping roof and a window that looked out over the little farm. It was a nice room. Cosy. One evening a few days into our stay I was up there while Mum, Deb and Doug watched a DVD that I wasn't allowed to see and didn't want to anyway. I was going through some annuals Doug had looked out for me, tatty old ones from when he was a kid, which weren't half as boring as you might expect. They were boys' annuals, but I wasn't into the stuff girls are expected to drool over, so I didn't mind. I'm not sold on pink, for one thing, and I hate – I mean *hate* – books about cute fairies and ponies and big-eyed pets. Stories that try to yank your heartstrings and make you go aaaaah and all warm and girlie inside. Yuk! Get a life, ladies.

Anyhoo. There I am reading this old annual in my attic at Deb and Doug's when all of a sudden this brilliant light fills the room from the window. Naturally, I jumped up and raced to the window, and from there I saw something bright falling out of the sky. My first thought was that it was a shooting star, but then I remembered the fair that had arrived that afternoon and was setting up on the Common. Probably something fairgroundy, I thought – till I realised that the light was a lot closer than something on the Common should be. Then the light died, and there was a dullish thud on the far side of the bonsai farm, at ground level.

I raced downstairs to tell the Golden Oldies what I'd seen. Ran into the lounge just as a bloke on the screen dropped his underpants.

'Good timing, Ange,' said Mum.

'Mum,' I said. 'Something just came down outside.'

'Outside?'

'In the garden.'

'The garden?'

'Yes, come and see.'

But her eyes had gone back to the screen. She was more interested in the starkers geezer in the film than anything I had to say. So was Deb. Doug was looking at the wallpaper.

'Angie…' My mother's way of reminding me that what they were watching wasn't suitable for a twelve year old.

I left them to it. Went to the back door, where

Dick the dog was dozing dismally on the doormat. One eye half opened when he heard me.

'Out of the way, Dick,' I said, slipping my outdoor shoes on.

He grunted gloomily and rolled off the mat. I pulled the door back and went out. The tall-as-a-three-year-old's-kneecap bonsai forest stretched before me. There was a path through the forest, which I walked along to the other side, and there I found the thing that had fallen to earth, glowing faintly, a purply sort of colour now. It was about sixty centimetres long, soft-looking, and bulgy like there was something inside it. It reminded me of a giant purse. I looked at the sky. If it had come from up there and wasn't a shooting star or from the fairground, it had to be from outer space. An alien craft. For very small extraterrestrials.

I tapped it with my foot.

'Hello? Anyone in there who wants to be taken to my leader?'

I don't know what I expected, but I certainly wasn't ready for what happened next. The purselike thing snapped open and quadrillions of multicoloured sparks flew out and covered my feet – along with a smell so absolutely disgusting that my nostrils tried to heal up.

The purse from outer space was an alien stink bomb!

But it wasn't *only* a stink bomb. I discovered this when my twinkling feet started to move in patterns, like they were trying to invent new dance steps. When I tried to make them stop I couldn't. I was dimly aware of the purse snapping shut as my feet danced me away between the bonsai trees, taking the ghastly stench with me. Only one other pair of eyes saw any of this: Dick the dog's, whose ragged little head peered around the half-open back door as I danced off.

In a jiff, I was dancing into the lane that runs alongside the farm. I commanded my feet to stop, but they just kept on, and on, and on, dancing me all over the lane like how to travel in a straight line had completely slipped their minds and toes. And with my feet dancing I found that my whole body also had to dance. Without the slightest input from my brain, my body pirouetted, jumped, came down on one foot, shuffled in circles, danced backwards, forwards and sideways. I even flipped over onto my hands a couple of times, which I'd never been able to do before, even when I was little.

Deb and Doug's place is on the edge of a small town, and this was the town my feet were dancing me towards. Towards and into. Because all the shops and most other places were shut now, it wasn't as busy as it would have been earlier, but there were still a few cars about, and people gazing into closed windows, and teens hanging out in groups. It was one of the teen gangs that noticed me first. When they saw me jitterbugging towards them, arms in the air, spinning round and round, they whistled and name-called, but when I passed them the smell of my twinkling feet hit them and they slammed their faces into their hands, which shut them up for a moment.

But even though I smelt really, really, *unbelievably* awful the teens must have thought it was some sort of act or jape, because in two ticks they were dancing along with me – very badly – flinging their arms and legs about and whoop-whoop-wah-hooing while squeezing their noses to keep the foul smell out. They soon ran out of steam, though, and found fresh walls and things to lean against with their hands in their pockets, but I had to carry on, go wherever my dancing feet took me. And on they went, weaving in and out of nothing, flipping me around, making me dance backwards, sideways, any way they fancied, like they were tuned in to some heavy rhythm that I was stone deaf to.

'You stink!' a little kid shouted at me as his mum hurried him by covering her nose.

'So do you!' I cried, leapfrogging a tramp sprawling in a doorway and landing on my toes like they were ballet points, before spinning away with my arms out to stop me losing my balance.

Eventually I managed to turn my feet back towards the farm, though I still couldn't stop them dancing. When I danced into the kitchen, where Mum, Doug and Deb were now, they didn't half look surprised, but seconds into the surprise they were overcome by the stench of my twinkling feet.

'Angie!' Mum shouted through her hanky.

'What?' I shouted back.

'What is that horrible smell? And why are you dancing? And why are your feet all sparkly?'

'The smell and the sparkle came from the alien

purse,' I said. 'Which also seems to be what's making my feet dance.'

'Angie Mint, stand still and talk SENSE!' Mum said sharply.

'I *can't* stand still,' I answered, leaping into the air and doing the splits.

'What was that about an alien purse?' Debra asked from inside her hands.

'The one that fell out of the sky behind the bonsais,' I told her.

Mum wasn't having any of this. 'I don't know what's got into you,' she said. 'But I want you up those stairs right away, in the shower. When I next see you I want you standing still and smelling *clean!*'

'Makes two of us!' I said, leaping up the stairs.

At first I couldn't stop dancing even in the shower, but the more I scrubbed myself with the loofah-on-a-stick the slower my feet moved, the less they twinkled. Bad as it was, I'd kind of got used to the smell by this time, so I wasn't sure if I'd washed it completely away, and when I'd dried myself and put on my jimmy-jams I went downstairs to ask. *Walked* down. I had control of my feet again!

'Do I still honk?' I asked Mum.

She sniffed. 'Don't seem to.'

'Before I took the shower you weren't in any doubt.'

She sniffed closer and harder. 'It's gone. And your feet are still.'

'Yeah. And twinkle-free.'

I thought of Jiggy McCue, who lives across the road from me. From the moment he could walk he'd jigged and danced around whenever it looked like the dung might hit the electric fan, and everyone was so used to it that we didn't notice it much any more. Now that own feet had stopped trying to find half a dozen grooves at once I realised how relieved Jig must be when he can stand still again. For the first time ever, I felt sorry for him having to put up with it all the time. Maybe I'll be nicer to him from now on, I thought. But then I thought, Will I heck. A girl has to have *some* fun.

Next morning I had a lie-in till about half nine. I would have stayed in bed longer, but Mum woke me to tell me she had to go to the shops and that

I wasn't to open the door to anyone while she was gone.

'Why? Where are Deb and Doug?'

'They're at the fairground, setting up a stall.'

'What, to sell bonsais?'

'Yes. They need to make what they can, poor things. Times are hard.'

When I heard the front door close behind her, I got up, dressed, went downstairs, grabbed a cereal bar from the kitchen, and took the path through the bonsai forest. The purse from outer space looked the worse for wear after a night on Earth, sort of saggy and dull. It must have sensed me, though, because while I stood there – not too close this time – it opened just a little, like a mouth about to speak. I jumped back to be on the safe side, but it didn't open any wider. Didn't seem able to.

I was trying to decide what to do about the purse when I realised that Dick the dog had followed me out.

'What do you make of this then, Dick?' I said.

'Make of what?' he answered, though it would have sounded more like 'Yip!' to an untrained ear.

'This. Our visitor from space.'

'Well, since you ask, I have an idea about that,' he said doggily.

'You do?'

'Yeah. I mean woof. You know how when you took a shower, you washed the twinkly-stink away and stopped dancing?'

'Yes…'

'Well, maybe the purse doesn't like water. Maybe water will put it out of business permanently.'

'So what do you have in mind?'

'This,' said Dick, trotting boldly forward, cocking a hind leg, and spraying it all over.

The purse didn't react right away, but when it did it wasn't the way either of us might have expected. It lost its saggy look, its colour returned, it sprang open, and a shower of multicoloured sparks flew out and covered little Dick from head to tail and back again. When this was done the purse slammed shut again, like it had done its job, but by then the smell had hit me. The utterly gross odour that twinkily covered Dick was so powerful that I had to make a real effort to stiffen my knees before they buckled under me. The stink bothered me more than it seemed to bother him, but maybe that's because dogs stick their noses into all sorts of things that humans wouldn't go near without a diver's helmet and a periscope.

Then Dick's feet started to move. At first they didn't seem to know what to do, but after a bit of confusion all four of his paws began to lift and dart and shuffle, and when they'd got in step with one another they danced him through the bonsais, two steps this way, two that, and up and back and round and round.

Wow, could that little dog dance!

Dick was more or less sticking to the path through the forest, but I didn't want to risk Deb and Doug's crop, so I ran to the house for his leash. Racing back, I held my breath while I slipped it round his neck, taking care not to touch him in case he was contagious.

'C'mon, Dick. You need to dance this off before the Oldies see and smell you and have you fast-tracked to doggie heaven.'

All I could do was hold on to the leash while Dick danced doggedly ahead of me along the lane. At the end, you had a choice of two directions – to town, where I definitely didn't want to be seen after last night, or the Common, where there's lots of open space and fewer people. Dick's feet seemed to like the town idea, but mine were bigger and I tugged him the other way.

When he first started dancing, Dick's eyes had been like big marbles as he cranked his head around and down to see what his feet were playing at. But he was adapting nicely now, and he gave these bright little barks as he danced along, wagging his tail for the first time ever while I was around. The few people we passed stared at dancing Dick as we approached, but as we drew near they shoved their faces in their hands or hankies or under their coats and reeled away.

There was something else too. Something different about the way Dick danced from the way I had. Maybe it was because he'd got a full-body dose of twinkly-stink rather than just a foot dose, but whenever we came to a tree his legs danced towards it and up it as far as the leash would let him – *and he didn't fall off*! When he'd danced as high as he could he danced back down, and did the same thing at the next tree, and the next, and so on, up and down each one in turn, all the way to the Common – where the fair was setting up. I smacked my forehead. With all this stuff with Dick going on I'd completely forgotten about the fair. It wasn't due to open for a few hours yet but members of the public were already mooching around it.

'You can't be seen here,' I said to Dick. 'Or smelt. Come on!'

But just as I turned away expecting him to follow, some fairground techie decided to test the music system. As *Bat Out of Hell* cranked up, Dick's feet got excited. So excited that he jerked the leash out of my hand and belted off towards the music.

'Dick! Dick! Come back! Stop!'

He didn't come back. He didn't stop. He didn't even pause. Which meant I had to go after him. A few people noticed us, but they probably thought he was just an escaped dog being chased by his minder. The only thing that stretched their necks was that he was twinkling from snout to tail-end. But then he passed them and they got a noseful of him and they clapped their hands

115

over their noses in disbelief.

The music was blasting out of several speakers around the site, so when he reached the fairground, Dick's feet didn't know which way to take him. What they did know was that they needed to boogie. The trees must have given them a taste for vertical dancing because they scampered towards the nearest thing that could be danced up – the Climbing Wall. Dick went up the wall and across it, and down it, and up it again, and over the top, and down the other side, yapping happily. A crowd formed as amazed eyes followed his progress, and every time he danced nearer the ground everyone leaned back with a gasp and squeezed their nostrils.

The only person who wasn't too gobsmacked to do anything but gawp was the man who ran the wall. 'Whose hound is that?' he roared. 'Get it off my apparatus!'

I was just going to admit that Dick belonged to me – sort of – when someone else claimed him.

'He's ours!'

In all the excitement I hadn't noticed Deb and Doug setting up their bonsai stall nearby.

'Angie! What's Dick doing here?' Deb shouted over the music. 'And how is he staying up on that wall? And why is he all sparkly? And is he...*dancing*?!'

Why do adults have so many questions all the time? Why can't they just accept what they see, like kids do?

'It's the alien purse that landed in your garden!' I shouted back.

'Alien purse?'

'I told you about it last night! It made me dance then! Today it's making Dick!'

While Deb and I were having this shouty chat, Doug was climbing the wall, handhold by handhold, foothold by foothold, trying to catch hold of Dick's flailing leash. At last he managed to grab it and started down, lugging the lively little dog after him. This can't have been easy because he had to keep pausing to take a deep breath in his armpit as a change from the revolting stink of Dick.

They reached the ground just as the song ended and silence returned, but twinkly Dick went right on dancing – and stinking. The crowd pulled back, smothering their noses. The night before, when the smell was on me, I'd got used to it, but now that it was on Dick I couldn't stand it any more than anyone else could. When I noticed that Deb had been using some of her fancy bonsai-wood clothes-pegs to pin a cloth to the stall they were setting up, I went over and pulled one off and clipped it on my nose. It squeezed my nostrils snugly but it didn't hurt, and it cut out the smell completely. I grabbed some more pegs and went back to Deb and Doug, who were talking to a man I didn't know. All three humans were holding their noses as they talked, which made them sound and look pretty funny. When Deb saw the peg on mine she didn't need persuading to put one on hers.

'Whew, that's better!' she gasped.

I offered a peg to Doug, who took it and clipped it on his nose. Instantly free of Stench of Dick he nodded appreciatively.

'Care for one?' Deb asked the man I didn't know.

He also took a peg, and when he put it on he looked instantly grateful. It turned out that he was the owner of the fairground and that he was knocked out by Dick's dancing on the Climbing Wall. He said that a dancing dog was cool enough, but a dog that could defy gravity into the bargain could be one of the big draws of the fair, and that people would pay to see such a phenomenon. Doug wasn't sure about this.

'We don't know how he's doing it,' he said.

'Angie seems to,' said Deb.

Doug turned to me. 'You do?'

I nodded, and would have explained, but Deb said they had to check it out for themselves before they talked about it any further. She told the fairground boss that we'd be back, and the three of us, led by dancing Dick, headed for home, pegs still on noses. It was hard to keep Dick on the ground now he'd discovered that he could dance up anything. He danced up more trees, and fences, and along the tops of brick walls, yapping joyfully the whole time

'I never saw him so cheerful,' Doug said.

'Maybe that vet was onto something after all,' said Deb.

'Like what?'

'Dick being in the wrong body. Maybe he did live before. As a dancer!'

Mum was home when we got back, fretting

119

about me not being there and not even leaving a note to say where I'd gone. But when Deb told her about Dick she was fascinated, and this time she paid attention when I repeated the story about the purse from Mars or wherever. We shut Dick in the house (still dancing) and the four of us trooped through the bonsai farm to look at the purse. I warned them not to stand too close unless they too wanted to dance like stink and be unable to stop.

'What makes you think it's from outer space?' Deb asked me.

'I saw it fall out of the sky.'

'Not exactly a flying saucer, is it?' Mum said.

'I never believed in those things anyway,' said Doug.

'But you can believe in a flying purse?'

'Only because I'm looking at it and Angie saw it come down.'

'Have you looked inside it?' Mum asked me.

'Inside it?'

'For little green men or…whatever.'

'The only thing I know that's inside it is sparkly stuff that makes you dance and smell bad,' I said.

'Maybe it's an unmanned mission,' Deb suggested. 'To check out the lie of the land, see what the residents of Earth are like, that sort of thing.'

'We have more important things to think about than that,' said Doug. 'Such as what we're going to do about the fairground boss. I mean it's all very well him saying we could make money with a gravity-defying dancing dog, but how do we know Dick'll keep on doing it? Who's to say it won't wear off?'

'True,' said Deb. 'But if he does keep dancing, we might make a little extra cash today.'

'People aren't going to pay to watch Dick dance if they have to hold their noses,' said Mum.

'They won't have to hold their noses,' I said. 'We sell them Deb's pegs. They can go as close as they like then.'

'They're clothes-pegs, not nose-pegs,' said Debra.

I shook my head. 'As far as your public's concerned, these are special pegs, made specifically to keep out the smell of Dick.'

'You really think people will put them on their noses?'

121

'You did. Doug did. The fairground man did.'

'Yes, but we didn't have to pay.'

'Pegs or no pegs,' Mum said, 'none of this will work if Dick stops dancing. Angie stopped, so why wouldn't he?'

'I only stopped when I took a shower,' I reminded her.

Doug laughed. 'Don't let's give Dick a shower then, eh?'

'You know,' I mused, 'it might only be domestic water that kills the smell...' They all looked at me. 'There's something I need to test,' I said. 'Is there a watering can about?'

'Garden shed,' said Doug.

I went to the shed and half-filled the watering can – one of those old-fashioned long-necked jobs. I came back with it and sprayed the alien purse. It immediately shrivelled and lost some of its colour.

'Just as I thought,' I said. 'It can't handle fresh water. Maybe it doesn't have purified water on its home planet. But there's another kind of water that it *does* like...'

'Another kind?' said Mum.

'Yes. Dick-pee.'

'Uh?'

I told them about Dick cocking his leg over the purse and how it instantly became more healthy and opened and twinkly-stunk him.

'So you think that if Dick wees over the purse it'll revive again and squirt him with fresh stinky twinkles?' Deb asked.

'Everything's pointing that way,' I said.

'Well, let's hope so,' said Doug. 'The fair opens at midday and we have to be there to either sell bonsais or run a dancing dog show.'

Dick didn't let us down. He was the absolute hit of the fair that day. The crowds we got! When the fairground boss saw how popular Dick was he got some of his men to erect a seven foot high screen so no one could see what was occurring on the other side without paying. Then he stood at the entrance with a megaphone and yelled 'Oyez, Oyez, roll up and see the dancing dog!' Punters were warned about the smell so there'd be no comebacks and given the option of buying a bonsai peg or putting up with it. The first people in didn't buy the pegs,

123

but almost at once they were staggering out and paying for them before diving back in to catch the rest of the show.

Before long, Doug and the fairground boss – Jim Wilder – had got the enterprise truly sorted. Mr Wilder had tickets run off on a laptop, and five minute performances were offered. Of course, Dick couldn't stop dancing during the intervals, but while new queues formed between performances I looked after him in a small tent nearby, soft-talked him, patted him, gave him water to drink and all.

While the first shows were going on, Mr Wilder got his carpenters to cobble together a set of steps and a two-metre-high 'wall' for Dick to dance up and over. Dick obliged, but towards the end of the afternoon he lost some of his twinkle and his feet weren't dancing quite as brilliantly as before, so I told Deb and Doug that we should shut up shop, and we did. People who'd heard about the gravity-defying dancing dog were disappointed not to have seen him, but Mr Wilder told them to come back tomorrow, when Dick would be refreshed.

'Hope he is,' Doug muttered. 'That dog could make us a packet.'

Mum and I left him and Deb to pack everything away and walked Dick home. Walked? He danced all the way, dog-tired as he was.

When Deb and Doug came home they were over the moon about the way things had gone. They'd taken more money than they'd imagined possible with bonsai trees. Dick was snoozing in his basket by this time. He'd stopped twinkling and his little legs had finally stopped dancing. The smell had worn off too. Turned out that you didn't need to take a shower. You just had to wait.

'Clever little fella,' Doug said, kneeling down and stroking Dick's dozing head. 'Pull off the same stunt all week and it'll be a golden bone for you the day the fair leaves town.'

That night we put up a small tent over the alien purse in case it rained. It didn't rain, but we weren't sure how fit it would be after another night on Earth. Dick seemed keen to find out next morning, and I went with him. Inside the tent, we found the purse all crimpy and dull again. When Dick cocked his leg and started to spray it,

I backed out but held one of the tent flaps so I could see in. The purse revived almost at once, snapped open, all-overed Dick with twinkly-stink, and right away he was a waggy-tailed dancing dog that you couldn't bear to be near without a bonsai peg on your nose.

Dick danced for his adoring public every day until it was time for the fair to move on. Mr Wilder tried to persuade Deb and Doug to join the fair and travel with him — Dick too, of course — but they saw a chance to go it alone. They did too. They gave up bonsai farming and bought an old gypsy caravan and an old gypsy horse and took the show on the road, with the tented purse riding in a trailer behind.

Dick is quite famous now. He's even been on TV, dancing up mini-replicas of the Empire State Building and Eiffel Tower. He paw-prints autograph books all the time. You might wonder how he feels about all this dancing and stinking and attention and all. You might even think it's cruel to make an act of him. Cruel? I don't think so. You just have to look at him. These days, Dick bounces around even when he's not been sprayed by the purse from outer space. He loves his life now, you can tell. Absolutely loves it. You never saw such a happy little dog. Or such a smelly one.

Angie Mint

FUR AND FEATHERS:
MY HARD LIFE

by
Stallone the Cat

Translated from the original Catese by
Renfrew Ferball-Clore, P.A.W., H.I.S.S.
of the Royal Feline Translation Institute, I.o.W.

All right, so I'm a Cat. Get over it. You're no better than me just because you're bigger. Size isn't everything. And who's got the most legs, you or me? And fur and a tail? Not you. Get out of that.

I'm going to tell you my story now. My personal story. All you have to do is sit quiet and pin your ears back. Think you can manage that? All right then, let's go.

My eyes were closed for quite a time after I was born, so my earliest memory is of complete darkness. I felt movement all about me, heard sounds, smelt things, but that was it. I must have been a curious kitten, though, because the day my legs were strong enough to support me I was off, feeling my way about, bumping into things, knocking things over, sniffing – until the Cat who must have been my mother snatched me up and took me back to where she thought I ought to be.

When my eyes finally opened I saw that I wasn't

the only newborn. There were three others, and we were in a shadowy room full of garden tools and equipment. A shed. There were shelves too, with boxes and bottles and balls of string on them, and a spider dangling on a long thread. All these things – the ones I could reach anyway – demanded to be examined at close quarters, so examine them I did. I was the only one who seemed interested. The others would get up and stretch occasionally, sniff around a little, then curl up again and doze, or just lie there quietly.

The big mother Cat was away most of every day. She came and went through a high window. When she returned she would tell me off for wandering about and being nosy. She was away the day I left home. I was examining the grass box behind the lawnmower when the door flew back and a No-Tail came in – the first No-Tail I'd seen. And what a huge, loud creature he was! I could only tremble in my hiding place as he shouted and scooped up the other three kittens and carried them off. But he left the door open. The door had never been open before. I waited till there was no more sound and crept to it. I looked out. So much space! So much to inspect!

And off I went, to see what I could see and sniff and taste.

The world turned out to be a loud and frightening place. I had to hide very often from the giant No-Tails and their big noisy vehicles, and find food where I could. But I soon learnt what to approach and what to keep away from. As I learnt, time passed and I grew bigger, more careful, more cunning. I was almost as big as I am now when I came to Brook Farm. There were a lot of strange animals on the farm. Most of them left me alone – even the Dog after a bit of barking when we first met. Once he got used to my presence he just nodded when we came upon one another and walked on by.

Sometimes I jumped up onto a barrel outside the farmhouse and peered in the window. I liked the way it looked in there. Comfortable, dry, peaceful. I went into the house three times, but the first two times left in a hurry when I heard sounds from another room. The third time I got as far as the kitchen, and jumped onto the table. There was food there. I tucked in. Delicious! I was enjoying my meal so much that I didn't hear Mr Brook the farmer come in, but then a hand slapped my head and I flew off the table and fled.

That was the last time I went into the house, though I did try again. The other times it was guarded by a very large, very angry Goose. Her name was Hetty. She was the only creature Mr Brook would allow inside. Maybe that was why Hetty thought she was special. She acted like it was her farm, strutting about and hissing and raising her wings if anyone got in her way. Everyone except Mr Brook was scared of her, even the Pigs and Horses. She took a dislike to me at first sight – possibly because I wasn't one of the farm animals – and flew at me furiously whenever she saw me. She didn't like No-Tail visitors either. When Men came to the farm she would bar the way until Mr Brook ordered her away.

It was a run-down and smelly old farm, all tumbledown buildings with sagging roofs, but it was somewhere to live. I never starved there thanks to the food put out for the animals. There was always somewhere to shelter at night too, so it wasn't a bad life as long as I kept out of Hetty's way. But after a while things changed. Trucks and lorries came and began to take animals and machinery away, and the old barns were knocked down. Soon the house was the only building still standing and I was the only creature left, not counting Hetty and Mr Brook. Hetty was angrier than ever now, and not just with me. She didn't like the changes, or the strangers. More and more Men came, digging up the fields, laying concrete, putting tall poles in the ground and building walls between them. There weren't as many places for me to shelter now, and food was scarcer than it had been because the Men didn't leave much. Sometimes they dropped bits that they were eating, but if they caught me nibbling them they aimed a boot at me.

But it wasn't the new Men who forced me off the farm. The day that happened, I was quietly lapping up some tea one of them had thrown away when Hetty jumped me from behind. Then she was chasing me while the Men cheered. She chased me all the way to the outer limits of the farm, and when I turned round at last I saw her standing there, legs spread, hissing threateningly, daring me to return.

I had nowhere to go, no idea what to do next, but just then a truck started up nearby. I jumped up onto it and buried myself under some smelly old sacks. The truck moved off, bumped over a cattle grid, and carried me away from that bad-tempered farmyard Goose.

I don't know how far we travelled, but the jolts and jerks of the truck must have made me drowsy, and I didn't wake until it came to a halt. I peeked out from my cover. It was nearly dark. When Men lowered the tailgate and began to unload the equipment on the truck, I flew out and made them jump. My paws hit the ground and I raced across a big untidy yard and through an open gate. I didn't stop till I was well away from there. All about me now were tall, dark buildings, and words and shapes painted on dirty walls, and mess and litter on the pavements and road. I didn't like it there at all. I put my nose in the air and walked away.

So began my time in the town. It wasn't a good time. All I wanted was a bit of food from some kitchen, somewhere cosy to lie at night, but No-Tails threw things at me or yelled at me for no reason. One time I came upon a building that had tables outside it, and No-Tails sitting at them, drinking and talking. When a Man got up from one of the tables and went into the building, I thought I would taste his drink. I jumped up onto the table and lapped the foamy stuff in his big glass. It was very bitter but I was thirsty and I drank as much as I could before the Man returned and took a swipe at me. I jumped down, but as I ran away my legs tripped over one another and my head went all spinny, and I sat down sharply. The Man whose drink I'd tried ran up and kicked me. Normally I would have shot off without delay, but I couldn't even stand. It was very strange and worrying. The Man drew his foot back to kick me again, and he would have, but a Woman came just in time and pulled him away.

The worst thing that happened to me in the town was the night of the big lights and bangs. There were whizzes and howls in the sky, and fur-raising whistles, and it was very frightening. I found a hiding place under a bridge by a canal. There were tin cans and bottles everywhere, and food wrappers, and the water smelt bad, and there were rats. I've never liked rats. I curled up against an old box, trembling. What was going on in the world? What were the flying lights and loud noises all about?

Suddenly there were voices, and No-Tail shapes standing just outside the bridge. Boys. With a torch.

'Hey! Look! Whassat?'

The torch found me. Its light dazzled me. But I didn't dare run. The whiz-bang-whistles still filled the night out there. The Boys came closer, whispering. Then—

'Grab it!'

—they pounced on me. They held me so tight that I couldn't wriggle free, but when one of them squeezed my neck I scratched him. He yelled.

'I'll kill the thing!'

Then I was bundled into a smelly sack they found, and the open end was closed, and it was dark, and there was a thump which jarred every bone in my body, and the sack was being dragged along the rough path beside the canal with me inside. It was a long and painful journey, but eventually we came to a halt and I could see light, flickering light, through tiny holes in the material.

Then the sack was lifted up, and swung about, and there were roars of laughter as the sack went flying. It landed on something sharp and brittle that cracked and gave way, and I felt heat. The heat grew and grew, and I smelt smoke, and I couldn't breathe properly. Then the sack began to smoulder. I became frantic, but however much I clawed and kicked I couldn't break out.

Suddenly there were more shouts, not Boy shouts this time, and the sack was lifted up and taken away from the heat. When it was set down and opened I peered out at a fire as huge as could be, with a Man in a chair on the top of it. No-Tail Men and Women were gathered round, staring down at me. Some of them shouted at the Boys who had put me in the sack and thrown it on the fire with me inside, and the Boys stalked off, also shouting. Hands began to pat my hottest side, which was smoking a little, but I spat at them and ran between No-Tail arms and legs. Away I went, putting them and the huge fire and the Man on a chair behind me.

I stayed hot and smoky until I found a good puddle to roll in. When I licked my side I found that some of my fur was gone and the skin was very tender. I sought a quiet place in which to recover from my ordeal and stayed there for some days and nights, not even venturing out to find food. While there I thought back to how easy life had been at the farm before that Goose drove me out. If not for Hetty, I might be there to this day, I thought, instead of crouching here nursing injuries. I wished I could see her now. I wouldn't run from her again. Oh no. Another time I would give her a piece of my mind. A piece of claw too.*

Months of skulking around followed. I had learnt that No-Tails were best avoided, but they were everywhere. How many times I had to run for my life in those long days! On a certain night, having eaten nothing of substance for an age, I followed a tempting aroma down an alley illuminated by a single lamp halfway along. There was a building at the end, and it was from there that the nice smells came. As I approached the building a Man came out and tipped scraps into one of the big black bins that stood by the door. I waited for him to go back inside before approaching the bins. They were very high. I was

---

* To learn what happened to Hetty after she drove our hero away, see *The Curse of the Poltergoose*.

about to jump up on one of them and try to knock its lid off when I noticed a few bits and pieces that had spilled out onto the ground. I got stuck in.

'Reeeeeaaaaawwwwwllllll.'

I looked up, a strip of bacon between my jaws. A pair of bright blue eyes stared at me from between the shadows of the bins.

'That's mine,' said the voice that belonged to the eyes.

'And mine,' said another voice, from behind me this time.

'And mine,' said a third, also behind me.

I looked over my shoulder. Two Cats bared their fangs at me.

'This is our alley,' said the first Cat, the blue-eyed one.

'We don't welcome strangers,' said the second.

'We teach them lessons,' said the third, slyly.

I gulped the bacon down and backed away. As I did so, I saw that there were many more of them, and all were glaring coldly at me.

'I'm hungry,' I said.

'Find your own eating place,' one Cat snarled.

'I would but—'

I'd backed into the wall. The Cats fanned out, fencing me in.

'He needs to be taught,' one of them purred.

'He needs to be hurt,' purred another.

'No, please,' I said. 'I didn't know this was your place. I'll go.'

'I don't think we can allow that.'

This came from the first Cat. Blue-eyes. The gang parted to let him through. In the light of the single lamp, I saw that he was unlike any Cat I'd seen before, sharp of muzzle, with large pointed ears, a thin pale-furred face, thin body. He was smaller than most of the others too, but it was clear that he was chief among them.

He stared at me for a long time, silent and unmoving, and when he'd stared his fill he withdrew and the others closed ranks once more and began to advance, slowly. I apologised for trespassing, but they weren't interested. They wanted blood, my blood, and when they were ready to take it they threw themselves at me, all of them at once, except Blue-eyes, who stood back to watch the conflict. Conflict? Not much of one, at first. The gang was in a spiteful mood, and I was this night's victim. They clawed me, they bit me, they tried to tear me sinew from sinew, and I could do nothing but protect myself as well as I could – until one of them made a big mistake. He bit my tail. The agony was great, but my anger was greater. I began to fight back.

And O, how I fought!

My blood was up, and no longer for the taking. Suddenly I had no fear for my safety. A terrible shrieking and wailing rose up around the bins of the alley as I inflicted wound after wound. Had there been fewer of them I would have driven them off, and some did run, but those who stayed were too many for me, even in my fury. I might not have escaped with my life if not for intervention from an unexpected quarter.

'Oi! You lot! Outta here! Scat! Scoot! Shoo!'

And water fell, a fine fat deluge of it, and my enemies scattered in all directions. Even Blue-Eyes made himself scarce.

'Yah, you too! Go! Go!'

The toe of a boot lifted me off the ground. When I came down I found that I could only run a little way before my legs folded, but Scrap Man did not

143

pursue me and I dragged myself towards the lights of the street. I stopped just before the end of the alley and checked my condition. There was blood in my mouth and on my flanks, I had two broken claws and a bitten ear, I felt pain in all parts of my body, and I was terribly weary. I sank to the ground and closed my eyes.

It was still dark when I stirred, sensing a presence. A pale mist had formed in front of me, and out of it stepped a Cat, limping badly. At first I thought it was one of the gang back for more, but then I noticed something different about this one. He glowed. Yes, glowed. All over. I'd never seen such a thing before and for a moment I just stared. But then I thought, glow or no glow, you're still a Cat. I wanted nothing to do with other Cats just then. I bared my fangs.

'Go away. I want to be alone.'

He did not go away. He looked down at me, lying there, and said, in a deeper voice than is usual for a Cat, 'I am the Shining One.'

'The what?' I said.

'The Shining One. The Counsellor of Injured Cats. I've come to comfort you in your darkest hour.'

'Not interested,' I snapped. 'Leave me be.'

'You sound angry, my young friend.'

'Angry? Me? No, I enjoy being mugged in dark alleys.'

'There's a good side to that,' said the so-called Shining One.

'Good side? Oh, that's nice to know. And here was I thinking that I'm lucky to have got away with my life.'

'The good side is the knowledge you've gained tonight.'

'Knowledge? What knowledge?'

'That packs of homeless Cats are jealous of their territories. You'll be more careful where you seek food from now on.'

'Pity you didn't tell me that before I went down there.'

'I couldn't come to you before. You weren't injured then.'

'I got burned a while back. Doesn't that count?'

'That was my night off.'

'Anyway, this is nothing,' I said, not wanting to appear weak in front of another Cat. 'A few scratches, that's all. I'll survive.'

'I believe you will,' he purred. 'You're toughening up. That's good. You'll need to be tough without a home.'

'What's all this "home" stuff?' I asked.

'You don't know what a home is?'

'Remind me.'

'Home is a building, with walls, windows, roofs, fires.'

'Don't talk to me about fires!' I hissed.

'Or radiators. Radiators are more common these days.'

'Look, are we done here?' I said. 'Nothing personal, but I don't want company right now.'

'I'll go as soon as I've told you how I got my second name.'

'Your second? How many names have you had?'

'Just the two. My first was Dylan, after the No-Tails took me in.'

Now the Shining One became thoughtful and began limping up and down in front of me. Viewed from the side I could see that he had just one hind leg. With no fourth paw to come down on it was more of a back-end hop than a limp.

'The Man of the house was away when my

siblings and I were born,' he said when at last he stopped pacing. 'I never knew my mother. I imagine she was a stray who left her newborns on the step where she gave birth to them. The Woman and Girl of that house took us in and looked after us, but when the Man returned he was angry and plunged us one after the other into a pail of water until our eyes ceased to open. I was the only one whose eyes would not stay shut, though I was dunked time and again. This seemed to excite the Girl—'

'Dad! This one doesn't want to die! Oh, let me keep him, let me keep him!'

'—who clasped me to her, wet as I was, and I was allowed to stay. She and the Woman made a great fuss of me and treated me well, but the Man never liked me. Men and Cats don't mix well in my experience. My leg is proof of that.'

'Your leg?'

'The one I lost.'

'How can you lose a leg? Legs are stuck on. They don't go wandering off on their own.'

'I was dozing in the sun one day, on the grass beside the front drive, and the Man backed his car out of the garage, ran it onto the grass, and crushed the leg. I believe he did it deliberately. The Woman and the Girl rushed me to the vet, who removed the shattered limb. After that I was known by another name.'

'Your second. Which is?'

'Tripod.'

His glowing whiskers quivered with emotion at this, and he fell silent again, staring at the ground. I waited for a minute, then asked if that was it.

He looked up. 'I'm sorry?'

'Your story. Have you finished it?'

'Yes, I suppose I have,' he said. 'I just have to give you the Closing Advice and I'll be off.'

'Closing Advice?'

'To carry with you as you go forth from this alley.'

I sighed. 'Go on then, give me the Closing Advice.'

'Steer clear of Men,' he said.

'I do,' I said.

'Don't trust them,' he said.

'I don't,' I said.

'Boys either. Same breed, only younger.'

'I wouldn't trust any Boy as far as he could throw me.'

'That's the spirit. And mind you don't weaken if one of them appears to be nicer than the others. They're all as bad as each other under the skin. Cats are nobler beasts than any No-Tail. Remember that. All that we Cats need No-Tails for is refreshment. And shelter if we can get it.'

'What about Women and Girls?'

'They're generally safer, but don't encourage them or they'll pamper you, and next thing you know you'll be domesticated. Always stay a little wild. It's the only way you can train them to respect you.'

'And Geese?'

'Geese?'

'They're violent. They drive you away from farms.'

'Well, they would,' Tripod said. 'They're Two-Legs, like the No-Tails, and feathered to boot. Even the little ones are a bit dodgy. Whenever I saw a Feathered One I would deal with it before it could deal with me. My advice to you is to do the same, to be on the safe side.'

'I'll try and remember that. Anything else?'

'No, that's about it.'

'Great. Er...how did you get this job anyway?'

'Counsellor to Injured Cats? Oh, I simply happened to be there at the right time. Feline Social Services (the FSS) had just decided that there should be such a position, and they offered it to me when I died.'

I gasped. 'When you died? You mean...'

His whiskers twitched. 'You didn't think I was still alive, did you? With this glow?'

'How did it happen?'

'How? I'm a little hazy on that actually.'

'Tell me what you know.'

'I thought you couldn't wait to get rid of me.'

'I can't, but I'm...curious.'

'Well,' he said slowly, 'I've always supposed that it was natural causes. I was getting on a bit, and hadn't been feeling too well for some time – I'd never felt quite as fit after I lost the leg – and one day I found a quiet spot under a bush to lie down and...well, next thing I knew I was being interviewed for this job.'

'Were many others interviewed for it?'

'A few. But I think I had an advantage over them. Who better, after all, than a dead three-legged Cat to counsel injured live Cats?'

'True,' I said. 'Are we done now?'

'We're done.'

'Well. Thanks. For the life story, the tips and all.'

'You're welcome,' said Tripod, the Shining One. 'I'll be off then.'

'Right. See you around.'

'Good luck, young Cat. You're going to need it in this harsh world. And if you remember nothing else of our little chat tonight remember this: a Cat is superior in every way to any mangy No-Tail.'

With that, he stepped back into the mist and was gone. The mist went with him.

'*Oh, Archie, look. Poor thing seems to be hurt.*'

'*Leave it, Bella, it's just a stray.*'

'*It's really been in the wars by the look of it.*'

'*I said leave it.*'

'*But it's so cold tonight. I think we should take care of it until it's better.*'

'*Oh, don't be ridiculous.*'

'*Just till it's well, Arch. Just till it's well.*'

I opened my eyes. (Must have closed them for

a minute after Tripod left me.) A pair of No-Tails were bending over me.

'There-there, kitty, it's all right, there-there, there-there.'

I was too weary to bother about them. I closed my eyes again, and when next I opened them I lay on a big piece of furniture, and the only sound was the ticking of a clock. It was so peaceful there, and it smelt nice, and I thought, 'Is this what the Shining One meant by home?'

But then the Man came in.

'Get off the furniture, you! Bella, I told you to keep this alley cat out of here!'

Knowing how unkind Men can be, I jumped down and ran from the room. I would have fled that house there and then if any of the doors to the world had been open. But they weren't. I was trapped.

I tried to keep out of the Man's way after that, but whenever he entered a room and saw me he would say something in a harsh way or raise a hand, even when I wasn't on the furniture. It was plain that he didn't want me there. The Woman was much kinder. She would often stroke me, and she fed me and gave me somewhere soft to sleep. The two of them would talk about me sometimes. I couldn't understand the ridiculous No-Tail sounds they made, but I always knew when they were talking about me because the Man would scowl my way. For some reason he got especially angry about me towards the end of my time there.

'No, I don't want to think of a name for him, Bella. I told you not to get attached to him. He's better now. Time for him to go.'

'Go? Oh, we can't let him go now.'

'We can and we're bloody well going to. If you don't put him out, I'll have him put down.'

'You'll do no such thing, Archie. But as your mind's made up...I wonder if Peg and the boy would like him? The boy's never had a pet.'

'Yes, he has. He's got a budgie.'

'Since when?'

'Coupla days ago.'

'I didn't know. Why doesn't anyone ever tell me anything?'

'It's a budgie, woman, not a Mercedes.'

'Anyway, a budgie's not much of a pet. I think the

McCue household will be thrilled to be presented with a cat. Let's surprise them.'

Before I knew it, I was packed into a box with a few tiny holes in the top and driven to this place where there were streets and streets of new houses that all looked the same.* They carried the box up the path of one of the houses and rang the bell. The door was opened and the box was put on the floor and the lid lifted. A new Woman and a Boy stood over me. I snarled at them.

'He doesn't seem very friendly, Mum.'

'It'll be the box, Jig. Cats don't like to be cooped up.'

I climbed out and went to give my new home the once-over. The Boy tailed me.

'Stop following me!' I snapped.

He didn't take the hint. He seemed to be trying to get on my good side. Talking in a soppy sort of way—

'Here puss, come to Jiggy, nice puss.'

—which did not win me over. If he thought I was going to be all chummy with him he had a whole bunch of other thinks coming.

A bit later, after the two who had dumped me here had gone, another Man came in. I knew right

---

* I discovered later that the houses were built on Brook Farm, though I never did find Mr Brook's house again.

away by his tone that we weren't going to get on.

'What's this?'

'It's a cat, Mel.'

'I can see that. What's it doing here?'

'Mum and Dad have been nursing him back to health. He was in a pretty bad way when they found him. They've given him to us.'

'They've what?'

'They thought we might like him.'

'They thought wrong. You know how I feel about cats.'

'He's a present. I could hardly turn him down, could I?'

'I can. Pass the phone.'

'No. He's staying. We're keeping him.'

'Over my dead body.'

'Jiggy, fetch the bread knife!'

The Man scowled at me and made some more of those silly mouth sounds that his kind use. I didn't like him at all. I hissed at him.

'Did you see that? That is one mean cat.'

'He's just shy. New surroundings. He'll settle in.'

'Yeah, well he'd better not settle near me. Does he have a name?'

'Mum said they haven't given him one. So it's up to us.'

'There's only one name for a mog as mean-looking as that. Stallone. We're going to call him Stallone.'

I didn't expect to enjoy living with this family, and I didn't, and still don't, but one good thing came out of moving in with them. Revenge on an old enemy. Sort of, anyway. In one room in the house there was a cage. In the cage there was a Feathered One. It wasn't white, and it was pretty small, but these were details. Whatever its colour and size, it was one of *her* kind, Hetty's, and therefore my enemy. The cage hung on a stand that stood near a table, so I had no trouble reaching it once my new No-Tails went upstairs that first night. I opened the cage door after a bit of fumbling, reached in, and...

Well, let's just say that vengeance is tasty.*

So there it is. My life story. It's not over yet, of course, though I don't expect my life to get any happier. Another hardship or enemy is bound to be waiting round the next corner. My No-Tails think of me as their pet, but they know nothing. I answer to the name they gave me so they'll keep feeding

---

* To hear Jiggy's take on this part of Stallone's story, see *The Toilet of Doom*.

me, that's all. Sometimes I even allow the Woman to tickle my front while I lie on my back with my legs in the air. She's the best of the bunch anyway. I let her know that I think this by bringing her a mouse from time to time. I know she appreciates my gifts because she immediately jumps onto a chair to cheer before telling the Man or Boy to put it somewhere nice for her to admire later.

I go out quite a bit, especially at night, to stretch my legs and check on the neighbourhood. I get into the occasional scrap with a tom trying to make a name for himself, but I always win. I didn't go through all those tough times to let another Cat think he's better than me.

You No-Tails had better watch your step too. I'm Stallone, King Cat of the Brook Farm Estate. This is my territory. Step out of line and I'll come for you, claws out, fur flying.

Got that? Good. Now purr off, I have curtains to climb.

SHELLING PEES

by
Jiggy McCue

The only difference between my mother's belly and our garden shed was that one had wooden walls, a bumpy green roof, and a wheelbarrow inside it. What I mean is, her tum was huge. That sunny Thursday afternoon she was sitting on a stool outside the back door with the washing-up bowl between her feet, doing something she used to do with her grandmother when she (Mum) was a kid. She'd been coming over all nostalgic for her childhood lately. Going all misty-eyed and saying 'when I was a girl' and telling us about something that happened back then, never noticing Dad and me swooning with boredom in the background or lynching ourselves with invisible ropes.

Maybe it was because she was expecting a female-type baby that Mum had dug up all her old dolls and little-girl pictures and things, and stuck them around the spare room for when my sister arrived. Until now, ever since we moved into this house, the spare room hadn't been spare. We'd made sure of that. Packed it rigid with empty suitcases, boxes of junk, anything at all except a bed so people wouldn't be able to come and stay with us. But because the baby was due soon, Dad and I had had to clear the room out, which meant dumping a lot of stuff at the council tip, forcing other stuff up into the loft through the foot-square hole in the bathroom ceiling, and shoving the rest under my bed, which I thought was a bit of a liberty personally.

My mother wasn't what you might call elegant these days. 'It comes with the territory,' she said when Dad commented on this.

'What territory?' he asked.

'Pregnancy!' she snarled, and threw the thing she was reading at his head. The thing was the script of a play called *How to Murder Your Husband*.

I'd better explain why she was reading a script. Just before she got herself preggers, Mum saw this ad in the free paper that's rammed through our letter box every week whether we want it or not, and she got all excited. What excited her was that the local amateur dramatics group were looking for new people and she was tempted to apply because she used to love Drama at school, she said. When Dad heard that she fancied the idea of playing other people he said that he could do with a change, so go for it, and she did. Unfortunately, all that the am-dram types wanted new people for was to help with the scenery and stuff, so Mum was kind of disappointed. But she joined them anyway, hoping they would eventually see that she was our town's answer to Angelina Jolie or someone. So far they hadn't cottoned on to her amazing talent, but she was still hoping, and reading all the scripts she could lay her hands on, even though the only part she could play now was the Matterhorn (a mountain).

Mum had decided to dress for the real-life role of mother-to-be and kit herself out with a set of huge dresses and romper-suits from a Bloomin' Massive catalogue. The Thursday afternoon I'm talking about here, she was wearing one of the rompers, a purple one, which made her look like the Tellytubby with the stupid triangle on his bonce. She was wearing this to shell peas in. She'd bought about ten kilos of peas still in their pods and was unzipping pod after pod and dropping the peas into the plastic washing-up bowl below.

'Why not buy frozen or tinned, like you usually do?' I asked when she told me to wedge the bowl between her feet because she couldn't stoop that far.

'Because this is the way my gran used to do it when I was little,' she replied. 'Why don't you get another stool and help me?'

'Um…because I don't want to?' I suggested.

'Come on, Jig, give it a try. Shelling peas is very calming.'

'I am calm. School-free days do that to me.'

'Try it anyway.'

So to humour her I got myself a stool and sat opposite her with a batch of unpodded peas and started shelling them too. And you know what? It *was* kind of calming, squeezing those plump green pods until their seams split, then running a finger or thumb along the neat row of little peas inside and tumbling them into the bowl. Also, and this was quite a bonus, they were terrific, I mean *terrific*, to scoff right out of the pod.

'Don't eat too many,' said Mum.

'But there are millions here,' I said.

'Still. Moderation, Jiggy. Moderation.'

Like I said, it was a school-free day, even though it was a Thursday in term-time and I wasn't unwell or even pretending to be. There was a one-day teachers' strike for more pay, more flexible hours, more public executions for bad kids and stuff. Given a vote I would have stuck my hand up for teachers to stay out for a year, but I wasn't asked. A single day wasn't fair anyway. Strikes were on all over the country that week and thousands of adults in all sorts of jobs were off work for much longer than a measly day, including my father. Dad had no complaints about his strike. Not only did it mean that he didn't have to go to the crummy new job Mum had found for him, but footballers were still playing. There was some big Cup thing going on in Insane Footie World, and every kick, swerve, header and hug was being televised and endlessly discussed, so he could glue himself to the screen all day long and actually *cheer* at strikes.

'Wish I could go on strike with this pregnancy,' Mum said when my father wandered out into the garden during half-time.

He leant down and patted the geodesic dome that used to be a stomach. 'Soon be over,' he said cheerfully.

'Oh yes. Then the screaming starts. And the violence.'

'Violence?'

'When I set about you with the strimmer for ruining my figure and putting me in such pain.'

'Blame the kid for that, not me,' Dad said.

I looked up from my peas. 'Don't bring me into this.'

He thumbed the Mum-Tum. 'The one in there.'

'Don't blame Swoozie either.'

'Swoozie?'

'I mean Suzie.'

What I knew and the Golden Oldies didn't was that although they were going to name her Suzie, as soon as she started to talk my little sis was going to call herself Swoozie because she wouldn't be able to say her proper name. I knew this because I'd met her before, sort of, when she was eight.*

'Have you read that booklet from the clinic yet?' my mother asked my father.

'What booklet?'

---

* To read about this see *The Iron, the Switch and the Broom Cupboard.*

'*Delivering for Dummies.*'

'Why would I?' he said. 'I won't be delivering her.'

Mum drove a grim thumb through a split pod of peas. 'You ought to at least know what *happens* at your own child's birth, Mel.'

'I know what happens. The brat pops out and keeps me awake night after night until you can train it to shut the hell up.'

'She's a she, not an it,' I said. That was my sister he was talking about. But Dad was already heading back to the telly.

He didn't make it. The front doorbell rang before he got there and Mum yelled at him to answer it. I heard him swear, then heard the door open and a garrotted sort of yelp followed by voices that froze Mum's podding hands. 'No,' she said. 'Can't be.'

But it was. When Dad came out again he was towing two super-tanned visitors, and he did not look delighted.

'Hello!' said Mum. (This wasn't said with much delight either.)

'Hello!' beamed the tanned visitors in perfect sync.

'But you're in Spain!'

'I don't think we are,' said her mother, who doubled as my gran.

For the record, my grandparents don't like to be called Gran, Grandma, Granddad, Grandpa or any of the other grandparenty-type names most families use. It would make them feel old, they say. From Day One I'm supposed to have called them Bella and Archie, but I hardly ever have, except maybe when I was too young to know better, because they're not first-name sort of people somehow.

'Well, wasn't that the plan?' Mum asked, still on the geriatric-hols-in-España theme.

'It was the *plan*,' Bella said, 'but ten days of relentless sunshine was more than enough for us, so we came home early.'

'But the weather was what you went there for!'

'Yeah, but there is a limit.' This was Archie. 'Day after day of the stuff can get a bit much. I don't know how the locals stand it. Any tea on the go? Love a cuppa. Whatcher...Jiggy?'

'Hello.'

Nice to be noticed at last, even if he wasn't a hundred per cent sure of my name. It's not just *my* name Archie has trouble remembering. Dad's is also a bit tricky for him. For both of them. It's always been the same. Me and Dad have never felt quite like members of our own family when my mother's parents are on the scene.

Now that I'd been brought to her attention, Bella gripped my cheeks and slapped my forehead with lips of steel. Then she went to Mum and hugged her very quickly and briefly, like she couldn't bear to hold her for long. 'You've put on weight, Peg,' she said. 'A lot of weight.'

'It happens during pregnancies,' said Mum.

'You're pregnant? At your age?'

Mum sighed. 'I told you. On the phone. Several times. And in an email.'

'Oh yes, rings a bell now you mention it. Not long to go, by the size of you.'

'No. Should all be over by the end of next week.'

While this conversation was taking place, Dad backed silently into the house. I was the only one to see him go.

'What are you two up to?' my gran asked her daughter and me.

'Shelling peas,' Mum said, in a way that said, 'Isn't it *obvious*?'

169

'My mother used to do that,' said Bella.

'I know.'

'There was some point to it back then. Now, though, what's wrong with frozen or tinned?'

'That's what I said,' I said.

'Nothing's wrong with them,' said Mum. 'It's just that I...'

She trailed off because her mother had stopped listening. I found this quite interesting because she – my mother – does that very thing with me, all the time.

Before we moved to the Brook Farm Estate my grandparents lived within easy reach of us by car and visited every so often, but then they retired and moved to the other end of the country, and we stopped seeing them so much. This suited Dad pretty well, and Mum was happier too because even she can't relax when they're about. She phoned them occasionally because she thought she ought to, but since they started jetting off and cruising all over the place and joining societies and things we seemed to have taken a bit of a back seat in their lives, which also suited Dad.

'Did we mention that we're gasping for the leaf

of the tea plant?' Archie asked, flopping into one of the garden chairs.

'Mel!' Mum bawled into the house. 'Make some tea, will you?!'

There was no reply.

'Mel!'

'What!' (His distant voice.)

'Tea! Make some, please!'

'I'm watching the match!'

'Watch it later!'

'It's an important game!'

'So record it and play it back in slow-motion for the rest of the decade! Tea!'

Dad didn't say anything else, but I knew that even now he was reaching for the remote to record the rest of the match. Doing as you're told is a way of life for the males of the McCue household. The only one who doesn't jump to it is Stallone. Nobody bosses Stallone around. He'd just wandered out to see who'd arrived, and when he saw my grandfather his fur went up and he stalked back the way he'd come. He's never been fond of Archie, probably because he used to live with him and Bella and they dumped him on us when they'd had enough of him.

'So,' Mum said, still podding the peas, like I was. 'To what do we owe this...pleasure?'

'We just stopped off on the way to some new friends,' Archie said. 'Met them at a Rotary do and promised to stay a few days next time we were in their vicinity. Live quite near here apparently. Strewth.'

'What?'

Archie tugged a crumpled piece of paper out of his shirt pocket. 'The address they gave us.' He read the piece of paper. 'Gawdelpus, Upyours Close, Strewth. Boy, will they be surprised to find *us* on their doorstep!'

One of Mum's eyes met one of mine. She seemed to be having trouble not smiling. 'This Strewth, it's...where exactly?'

'According to the map they drew for us,' Archie said, 'it shouldn't be much more than fifteen or twenty miles south of here.'

He flashed the scrap of paper. There was a sketch on it of a couple of people in a car with arrows ahead of it that ended at a big cross that might not have been a kiss.

'There are some disused coal pits about there...' Mum said.

'Well, he said to aim for the pits. Our driver'll probably know it.'

'Driver?'

'Character we met at the airport in Spain. Sat next to him on the plane and stayed with him all through Customs and the three-hour baggage search. Quiet sort of cove. Bit of a squint.'

'And he offered you a lift?' Mum asked.

Her dad winked at her. 'He let slip that he was coming this way, and didn't say much when we threw our cases in his boot, so yes, as good as. Just as well, since there seems to be some sort of transport strike on.'

'Not only transport. Just about everything.'

'Except football,' I said, still podding the peas.

'This man with the car,' Mum said to my sainted grandfather. 'He's waiting outside for you?'

'Yeah. Told him we wouldn't be more than half an hour, hour at the most, depending how long the damn tea takes to get here.'

'We only dropped in to bring you some pressies,' Bella said, dipping into a holiday-type carrier bag she had with her.

I looked up from my peas. 'Pressies?'

'From Tossa del Mar, where we were staying.' She took something out of the bag. 'This is for Marvin.'

'Mel,' said Mum.

'Sorry?'

'That's his name.'

'Whose?'

'Your son-in-law's.'

'Mel, Marvin, same difference,' Bella said.

'What...is that?' Mum was staring at the thing in her mother's hand.

'It's a reading light.'

'A reading light?'

It didn't look like a reading light. It looked like a cheap plastic model of a squatting woman in a green swimsuit. She had red hair and a pout.

'You slip a couple of AA batteries between her legs and her hair lights up,' Bella said. 'You'll have to buy the batteries.'

'Mel doesn't read,' Mum said faintly.

'Except the results on telly,' I said.

'And this is for you,' Bella said to my mother.

She took out a flat box with a bumpy surface and handed it over.

'It looks like a cigarette case,' Mum said.

'It is. Covered in genuine snakeskin.'

Mum put the box down in a hurry. 'I don't smoke. Never have.'

'Well if you ever take it up, you'll have something to put your cigs in,' Bella said brightly.

'Something covered in the skin of a once-living snake,' I added.

Mum shuddered and Bella dived into the bag for the last present.

'And here's yours,' she said to me, producing a stick of red rock and a seashell the size of the Hulk's fist.

'I didn't know they did rock in Spain,' I said, trying to sound pleased.

'Only in the tat touristo shops like the one we got this crap from,' Archie said.

'The rock has the name of the resort running through it,' Bella said. 'And you can hear the Mediterranean in the shell.'

I wanted to say, I don't like rock, with or without the name of a Spanish resort I've never

175

been to running through it, and why would I want to hear the Mediterranean on the Brook Farm Estate? But I didn't say that. I said, 'Thanks, I'll... treasure them.'

'Rock's not to be treasured, it's to be eaten,' she answered. 'Take a bite.'

Mum looked at me. She knows I'm not a rock person. 'Later. After tea. As a treat.'

'Mmm,' I said, hoping it sounded like I couldn't wait.

There was a spot of very boring chat about Spain, then Dad arrived with two mugs of tea.

'About time,' said Archie. 'We're parched here.'

'Couldn't you have used cups and saucers?' Mum said.

'Why?' said Dad. 'Have royalty come to visit or something?'

'Didn't you make one for me?'

'Didn't know you wanted one.'

Mum made a 'Huh!' sound and turned back to her parents. 'I expect the gentleman who drove you here would welcome some refreshment,' she said.

'Someone *drove* them here?' said Dad, like he was thinking, Where is he, I'll kill him.

My mother set aside her heap of unshelled peas and heaved herself off her stool. 'I'll go and see if he'd like a cup. Or mug,' she added, glaring at Dad.

As she waddled out, Dad slipped back to his precious game, leaving me alone with the aged grandfolk. There was a pause. When the pause started to get embarrassing (almost immediately) Bella lobbed the yawnworthy question that visiting Golden Oldies always ask the kids of the house when they haven't seen them for half an hour or so.

'Well, um…Jiggy. How's school?'

'Terrific,' I said. 'How's retirement?'

'Oh, you know.'

'Well, no, but never mind.'

Another pause. Bella stood looking at flowers, Archie sat in the garden chair with his hands behind his head, I podded peas.

Then Mum returned. 'No car out there,' she said.

'What?' said Archie.

'Just some suitcases by the gate.'

'What!' He leapt out of the chair and ran to the front door.

Yet another pause while two of us looked at two

177

others of us for something to do. Then we heard a thud. And a second thud. Archie dropping suitcases in the hall. When he came back out, his expression told us that this was not one of those days you write home about. Nor did his words, which were:

'The miserable git's abandoned us!'

Mum frowned. I knew what she was thinking. That if her parents didn't have a driver to take them on from here, we could be stuck with them for quite a bit longer than we wanted. But then I heard her brain go 'ping' as an idea occurred to her.

'Mel!' she yelled.

A little while later, my grandparents piled into our car with their luggage and Dad floored the accelerator and drove off in search of Strewth, which he knew and Mum knew and I knew didn't exist.

Once the smoke of the exhaust had cleared, I slipped over the road to see Pete and Angie. I handed Pete the stick of rock and Angie the seashell.

'Presents,' I said.

Angie looked at the shell suspiciously. 'Why are you giving us presents? You never give us presents, even on our birthdays.'

'That's a lie!' I said. 'I gave you one last birthday. A book token.'

'Yes, an uncashed one someone had given you, and you only gave me that because I bombarded you with text messages and notes in your school bag, and by writing the date in indelible ink on your hand while I twisted your arm behind your back.'

'This is joke rock, isn't it?' Pete said, holding the Spanish rock at arm's length like it was a stick of dynamite. 'It's gonna blow up in my face or give me blue lips or taste like something your cat dragged in.'

'If you must know,' I said, 'it's from my grandparents. So's the shell.'

'Why would your grandparents give us presents?' Angie wanted to know.

'They didn't. They gave them to me and I didn't want them, so I'm passing them on.'

She curled the Mint lip. 'Second-hand presents.

I should've known. Well, stuff 'em, McCue!'

She thrust the shell back in my hand.

'I'm keeping mine,' said Pete. Pete likes rock. He unwrapped the end, bit some off, started crunching.

'Did they send them?' Angie asked me.

'Did who send what?'

'The grandparents, the lousy presents.'

'No, they just turned up and handed them over.'

'When?'

'Little while ago.'

'Bet Mel was pleased to see them.' She knew how Dad felt about his in-laws.

'He's the only one that's still with them as it happens.'

'How come?'

'Mum told him to drive them somewhere and drop them.'

'What, like some gravel pit with a bullet between the eyes?'

'I bet that's crossed Dad's mind too.'

'I knew it was a joke,' said Pete suddenly.

He was scowling at the end of the bitten stick of rock.

'Whaddayamean?' I asked.

He showed me the lettering that went around the inside of the rock. One word. TOSSA. I shook my head – Pete never could spell – and took my unwanted shell from Tossa del Mar back home with me. Pete kept the rock even though he thought he'd been insulted by it.

Indoors, I started upstairs, intending to go to my room. Halfway, I noticed Stallone staring down at me from the top, like he thought I had no right to be there.

'Hi-ya, furballs,' I said as I got within a stair of his stare.

'Rrrrrr.' (Catese for 'Watch how you speak to me, kid.')

He didn't step aside as I reached him, of course, which meant I had to go round him. I started along the landing and was almost at my room when I heard Mum's voice from somewhere behind me.

'Jiggy, is that you?'

'No, it's Mr Potato Head from number 86.'

'Come here.'

'Where?'

'Bathroom. Quick!'

With a long-suffering sigh I about-turned and plodded towards the bathroom. Seeing where I was going, Stallone jumped into my path, then sauntered ahead of me, slow as you like and weaving from side to side to stop me getting by. When the two of us eventually got to the bathroom we found my romper-suited mother sitting on the side of the tub, which was filled with steaming bubbles.

'She kicked me!' she said, eyes glowing.

'Who?'

She pointed at her gigantic belly. 'Suzie.'

'She's kicked you before. Loads of times. What's the big deal?'

'She's never kicked me as hard as just now.'

'So what are you gonna do, ground her?'

'Oh!' she said.

'Now what?'

'She's done it again. Really hard. Feel, Jiggy, feel!'

She reached for the hand that didn't contain the Spanish shell. I pulled back.

'I'll give it a miss, if it's all the same to you and her,' I said.

'Oh, but you must, Jig. It's a wonderful thing.'

'To be kicked? Ten minutes on the footie field with Ryan'd knock the wonder out of your ancient head.'

But she went on and on about me feeling the kicking baby, and to keep her quiet I let her place my open mitt on her giant stomach.

'Not kicking now,' I said.

'Wait.'

I waited.

'Still not.'

'Maybe she can sense you.'

'Yes, Mother. She can sense that I'm not someone who gets a kick out of being kicked. Now if you don't mind, I'm going to my ooh!'

I said 'ooh!' a frac of a sec before I took my hand away, when a little foot inside the bulgy romper-suit thumped my palm. It wasn't the kick that made me say 'ooh', though. It was the electric-type shock that zapped my other hand at almost the exact same mo and made me drop the Spanish shell on Stallone's head. Stallone yelped and skedaddled, tail pointing at the ceiling like an incredibly long finger.

'Lively little soul, isn't she?' Mum said, thinking

it was the kick that'd made me drop the shell.

'Isn't she,' I said.

I picked the shell up a bit nervously, but there was no second shock. I carried it to my room and shut the door. I was a bit shaken if you want to know. Seashells don't usually dish out shocks, so why would I get one from this one? Curious now, I did something I'd sworn not to when the grandies gave it to me. I put the shell to my ear and listened to the sea. It wasn't the sea, of course. I've known since I read it in a comic way back that what you hear in a seashell is only the sounds around you caught inside and shifting about in there.

'Mediterranean phooey,' I said aloud.

And then I heard something else.

'*Where am I?*'

I think my eyebrows went up at this. But then they came down and I chuckled. Anyone who didn't know better might have thought they'd just heard a distant voice calling over the sea in the shell. That ruled me out. As it wasn't really the sea, it also couldn't be a human voice, stood to reason. I put the shell to my smirk.

'You're in a pea-green boat with an owl and a pussycat,' I said.

Then I put the shell to my ear again, and heard...

'What's a pea-green boat? What's an owl? What's a pussycat?'

I jerked the thing from my ear and looked at it. I'd definitely heard a reply. Hadn't I?

I was still thinking 'Hadn't I?' when I got this urgent urge to pee. I mean this really powerful *need*. I tossed the Tossa shell on the bed, hoofed out of the room, along the landing, into the bathroom, threw back the toilet seat, and gasped with relief as I emptied half the Mediterranean in the lavvy bowl. I was down to the last few drops and going 'Wooh!' when I heard a voice that wasn't from the shell (which was still in my bedroom).

'Couldn't you have waited till I finish here?' the voice said.

It was my mother. I glanced to my left. She was in the bath, with bubbles up to her chinny-chin-chin.

Dad returned a couple of hours later, alone and without luggage.

'What happened?' Mum asked him.

'Couldn't find that place, surprise-surprise,' he said.

'Strewth.'

'Yeah. And that wasn't your old man's most growled word as we drove round and round failing to find it. In the end he said, "Sod it, we'll have to go home." So I found this really tucked-away little country railway station for them to catch a train.'

'But the train drivers are on strike,' Mum said.

'Yeah. So are the station staff. But they don't know that. I went in on the pretext of finding out if any trains were running and when I came out I told them one was expected any time that would take them all the way home and that they had to buy the tickets on board.'

'You mean you lied to get shot of them.'

Dad grinned. 'Yep.'

'Quite a bright move for you,' said Mum.

'Thanks.'

'Of course, you realise that they'll ring us and start ranting as soon as they realise they've been conned.'

'Don't see how,' Dad said. 'There was a phone at the station, but someone had inconsiderately ripped it out of the wall.'

He winked at us as he said this.

'You're forgetting Dad's mobile,' Mum said.

My father's grin broadened. He took Archie's little mobile out of his pocket, and said, 'He very carelessly left it in the car.'

Next morning I jammed the Spanish shell into my school bag along with my books and other rubbish. I wanted to see if Pete and Angie would hear a voice too, though I hadn't dared put it anywhere near my own ears since yesterday. On the way to school I was about to tell them about the voice when Atkins caught up with us and wouldn't shove off in spite of the insults, so it wasn't until Maths that I got a chance to nudge Pete and show him the shell under my desk.

'I've seen it,' he whispered while Face-Ache Dakin droned on about fractions of nothing we were remotely interested in.

'I know you've seen it, but you need to listen to it.'

'No I don't.'

'You do. It's got a voice in it.'

'A voice?'

'Either that or I've really lost it.'

'You did that years ago, mate.'

'You two at the back there, would you mind waiting till break for a private chat?'

I glanced Face-Ache's way. 'We're on strike,' I said.

'What?'

'Well, if you can do it...'

'I'll give you a strike, young man.'

'Great. Can we go home now then?'

This got a titter or two, but not from Dakin, who had a humour bypass while he was still in his pram.

'Settle down, everyone, settle down,' he said. 'McCue, sit up straight and pay attention.'

I sat up straight(ish) but the attention thing wasn't so easy. Still, I gave it my best shot till someone started snoring. Then I heard my name again. I opened my eyes. Face-Ache was peering at me from the front of the room.

'Were you speaking to me, sir?'

'I was,' he said. 'I asked if we were keeping you awake.'

'Well, you are now,' I said.

He closed his own eyes like he'd decided to go for the forty winks option too. But he spoke at the same time, which I thought was pretty clever for a teacher. 'Tell me, McCue,' he said. 'What is it about this lesson that you find so easy to talk and sleep through?'

'You want the truth, sir?'

'I can't wait.'

'Well, it's the subject. Maths.'

He opened his eyes. 'Not fond of it, eh?'

'Not terrifically, no.'

'Do you think it might be more interesting outside in the corridor?'

'I don't know,' I said. 'You could go and give it a try.'

'I mean you.'

'Me what?'

'In the corridor.'

'You want me to go out to the corridor?'

'That's the idea, yes.'

'I won't learn much out there, sir.'

'Well, it can't be much less than you appear to be learning in here.'

189

'True,' I said. 'Can I take a chair?'

'Oh, you'd like a chair, would you? Would you also like a footstool and a television set?'

'That'd be cool. Thanks.'

The ridges that Face-Ache's forehead was built out of got even deeper. 'You think you're very funny, don't you, McCue?'

'I do my best,' I said modestly.

Hoots from the class. Dakin would make a terrific stooge.

'Just go outside,' he said wearily, 'and stand there till the lesson's over, then come and see me about your detention.'

'Detention? What detention?'

'The one I'm going to give you.'

'Oh, that one.'

I got to my feet.

'What's that you have there?' he asked.

'Where?'

'In your hand.'

'Nothing.'

'That is definitely not nothing. Show me.'

I waltzed to the front of the class and showed him the shell.

'Listen to it,' I said. 'See if you can hear anything.'

He scowled. 'I know exactly what I'll hear. You giving me lip for the umpteenth time in your career.'

'I'm not giving you lip, I'm just saying listen to the shell and see what you hear.'

'Give it to me.'

'You're going to give it a listen?'

'No, I'm going to confiscate it.'

'You like confiscating things, don't you?' I said. He snatched the shell. 'Rude to snatch,' I muttered.

'Go!' he roared.

I went. And stood in the corridor for as long as my little legs would take the weight, then slithered down the wall into a squat. I wouldn't have told Dakin – wouldn't have thought it possible – but it was even more boring out there on my own than in his lousy lesson.

When the bell eventually went, everyone filed out and I filed in to see the Man as instructed. The usual conversation followed, with him telling me off for not paying attention in class, and me saying, 'I can't help it, I try,' and him saying, 'Oh, you do, do you, it's news to me,' and giving me a note for my parents telling them that I would be staying behind next Tuesday after school.

'Can I have my shell?' I asked when all this was out of the way.

'You can have it at the end of the day.'

'But I need it now.'

'At the end of the *day*, McCue!'

In the playground I tracked down Angie and Pete and told them what I'd heard in the shell the day before. Pete corkscrewed the side of his head and flopped his tongue out the side of his mouth. Angie just stared at me blankly like she'd heard it all before, which she hadn't. We'd been through quite a lot together, but a voice in a seashell was absolutely new.

'You wait till I get it back after school,' I said. 'You're going to listen then, like it or not. Then you'll have to believe me.'

That was the plan, but like most of my plans it didn't go the way it should have done. When I went to the staff room at the end of the afternoon Dakin wasn't there yet, and by the time he turned up and handed back the shell (along with another lecture) Pete and Angie had gone on without me and I had to mooch home alone.

Mum and Dad weren't in as usual at that time, so I took the big bottle of SmartSave Cola and a monster bag of Squares to the living room and did a lightning flick through the channels. All the usual stuff for that time of day. Cartoons, hopeless kiddie progs hosted by twits with stupid hair, John Wayne acting in his sleep, charmless couples accusing one another of being mean for a cheering audience. I checked the digibox to see if Dad had recorded any late night stuff that I wasn't supposed to see. He had. I was quite enjoying it when Stallone strolled in.

'Hiya, Stall, whaddyamake of this then?'

'Rrrrrr.'

'Yeah, couldn't agree more.'

Then I thought, Hey, he's got ears, maybe they'll hear the voice in the shell. So I flipped the telly off – reluctantly, because *Sexcetera* was very educational viewing – and closed the door so he wouldn't stalk out the moment I tried to be friendly. Then I offered the hand that wasn't holding the shell.

'Here. Come to your beloved master.'

He snarled like he understood every word and didn't like one of them, but started slowly forward, paw by paw by paw by paw, obviously thinking that maybe he ought to check this out in case I had something nice for him in spite of being a male human. I reached out to stroke his head but he jerked his face up, fangs bared. I'd been expecting this, and I lifted my hand before he could get a piece of it, and in the same movement grabbed him by the scruff and slapped the shell over his nearest pointy ear and held it there while he squirmed in my vice-like grip.*

Then he went all still – froze, just like that – staring glassy-eyed at nothing. The stillness didn't last long, though. Suddenly his fur went up like something shocking had been plugged into his bum, he jerked his neck out of my hand and his ear from the shell, and raced to the door, which was closed. Faced with a barred exit, he began hurling himself around the room looking for an unbarred one. When he didn't find one he started throwing himself at the walls, one wall after another, like he was hoping one of them might be weak enough to

---

* Animal cruelty action groups have been informed. Ed.

break through. All I could do as he flew back and forth was cover my head and yell at him to take it easy. My soothing yells did not work. When all of a sudden he stopped hurling himself at walls and stood like a cat statue it wasn't because of anything I'd said.

'Stallone!' I cried. 'What are you *doing*?!'

What he was doing was peeing long and hard over my dad's favourite armchair.

I leapt to the door and yanked it. He was gone the moment there was a gap wide enough to squeeze through. I turned back to the room and stared at the steaming chair as scenarios scurried around my brain like a trapped cat. Dad *might* not flop into the chair as soon as he came in, Mum *might* not smell the piddled-on material with her super-sensitive nostrils when she wobbled through the door, but these were not things that could be counted on. What could be counted on was trouble. For me. When something ungood happens in our house, eyes always flip instantly to me, like whatever it is has to be my fault. I needed to put space between me and this chair, this room. Distance myself from the scene of the crime.

I plumped up the cushions I'd been leaning against, cleared away all other evidence that I'd been there – the cola bottle, some dropped crisps – and shot upstairs. In my room, door firmly closed, I looked at the shell, which fortunately I'd brought up with me or I'd have been looking at my hand. I guessed from Stallone's reaction that it wasn't the sea-like sounds that had boggled his tiny mind. No, he'd heard the Voice, and it had scared him furless. So. Proof that I wasn't the only one to have heard it. I took a breath and stuck the shell against my ear. I heard the sea-that-wasn't, but no voice. At first. Then, quite small, in the distance…

'I'm floating!'

I jerked the shell from my ear. I peered inside it. I turned it over. I sniffed it. I looked inside it again. It was just an ordinary seashell, nothing special at all. The kind they call a conch, I think. I was fairly certain that phoney sea sounds in conch shells don't usually come with free voices, but this one did.

I put it to my mouth. 'Hello?' Then I hung it back on my ear.

'*Who's that?*' the little voice replied.

I put the shell to my mouth – 'Er...Jiggy' – and back to my ear.

'*What's an er-jiggy?*'

Back to mouth. 'Just Jiggy. Who are you?'

'*I don't know. Why am I floating?*'

'Floating? You mean like on a sea?'

'*What's a sea?*'

'Well, it's water. Salt water. Lots of it. How do you know what floating is but not what sea is?'

'*You tell me,*' said the voice.

'Hang on,' I said. 'Gotta go!'

And I did. Super urgently. Like before, I only just made it to the bathroom, and once again gasped with relief as this really amazing amount of wee weed forth. The good news is that my mother wasn't in the bath watching this time.

'I was busy,' Pete said when I met him and Ange outside their house. I'd called an emergency Musketeer meeting.

'Busy or not,' I said, 'what's the first rule of the Musketeers?'

'I dunno. What?'

197

'Drop everything when another Musketeer says "One for all and all for lunch".'

'Oh, that. Stupid rule. One of yours, naturally.'

'All the rules are his,' said Angie.

'Someone has to make up the rules,' I said.

'We get enough rules at home and school without you slapping more on us,' said Pete.

'Who are you calling a moron?' I said.

'Can we speed this up, whatever it is?' Angie asked. 'I had to put *Friends* on hold.'

'*Friends*?' I said. 'You've seen every episode two twillion times.'

'I like *Friends*,' she said.

'Good. So maybe you can find a small window in your hectic schedule for this one.'

'Go on then, spit it out, what's up?'

I raised my hand. Showed them the shell.

Pete growled. 'Ah, not that again.'

'There's someone inside it,' I said. 'Someone's voice anyway.'

'Old news,' said Angie. 'Didn't believe it then, don't now.'

'It's true. I've heard it and Stallone's heard it. What I want to know is, can you two hear it?'

'Oh, give it here!' Pete said, snatching the shell and clapping it to his ear.

'Nothing,' he said almost immediately.

'You have to give it longer than that,' I told him.

'How long?'

'Till you hear a voice.'

He put the shell to his other ear. Held it there for a few more seconds.

'Nothing,' he said, handing it back.

'Nothing? Not even the sea?'

'Whooshing sound is all.'

'That's meant to be the sea.'

'And the police car.'

'Police car? You heard a police car in the shell?'

'Not in the shell, here, in the street. It went by while I was lugholing that thing.'

'I didn't hear it.'

'It didn't have its siren on.'

'They'll be scouting for secret smokers and vandals,' Angie said. 'And cranks who think seashells talk.'

I held the shell out to her. 'Give it a listen.'

'Pete didn't hear anything.'

'That's Pete. You try.'

She put it to her ear. 'Just the sea,' she said in a while.

'Say something into it.'

'Into the shell?'

'Yes.'

'Why?'

'Just say something.'

'Like what?'

'Like "Hello in there, can you hear me?"'

'Your mind's gone, McCue,' she said.

'Yeah, yeah. Do it.'

She tutted, but put her mouth to the shell. Then she said, in a pretend spooky voice, 'Is there anybody theeeeeeere?' Then she eared the shell again and gave it five. 'Nope,' she said when she'd heard enough of nothing.

I took the shell back. 'Maybe it's taking a break.'

'So am I,' said Pete, and started to go.

'Wait till I try it,' I said.

'You already tried it.'

'Yes. I did. Twice. And it happened both times. Now I want to try it while you're here so you'll know I'm not making it up.'

'OK, but make it quick, I have a life to lead.'

I put the shell to my ear. Heard the sea-sound, and...

'Where have you been? I've been bobbing about here for ages waiting for you to come back.'

'It's there!' I said to P & A.

Little frowns appeared between all four of their eyes like they were wondering if maybe I wasn't fooling after all. Then Angie took the shell back and jammed it against her ear. 'What's it sound like?' she said after a pause or two.

'Like a voice.'

'Well I can't hear it.' She handed it back.

I put the shell to my mouth. 'Hello?' Then to my ear. And...

'Why do you keep going away in the middle of a conversation?'

'It's still there!' I said.

'It wasn't for me,' said Angie.

I was starting to need a widdle, but I valiantly mouthed the shell. 'Did you hear someone else talk to you just now?' I said to it.

'No. Did someone?'

'Yes – Angie.'

'What's an angie?'

201

'It's a sort of girl.'

'*What's a girl?*'

The need to pee was already getting serious. I crossed my legs as well as I could while standing, and bent over a little.

'It wants to know what a girl is,' I said to Angie.

'Often wonder that myself,' said Pete.

Angie heeled his toe, hard. 'A girl is a superior being and don't you forget it,' she said while he yelled with pain. 'Jig, do you need to go somewhere?'

I did, badly, but this voice business had to be sorted before anyone, me included, went anywhere. Clutching my lower regions with my free hand, I spoke into the shell again.

'Did you say something to Stallone back at the house?'

'*What's a house?*' the voice asked. '*What's a stallone?*'

'A house is where people live and Stallone's my cat.'

'*What's a cat?*'

'You don't know much, do you? Listen, can you hold on a minute?'

'*Why, you're not going again, are you?*'

'I have to. I mean I really have to. Hang on, you two, I need your toilet.'

The last bit was to Pete and Angie, but I was too late. They'd just gone into their house and closed the door. I pocketed the shell and rushed to the letter flap, which I lifted.

'THIS IS AN EMERGENCY!' I screamed through the gap.

Pete's eyes appeared on the other side. 'Your whole life's an emergency, McCue. Save the fairy tales for Atkins or some other dumpling brain.'

The eyes removed themselves from the gap. And that was that. I straightened up. Glanced across the road. My house was a full ten second sprint away. Ten seconds! Could I hold it in that long?

I sprinted over the road (well, hobbled fast) with one hand gripping hard while my other felt in a pocket for my front door key.

No key.

I switched hands and groped in another pocket. Also empty.

I groaned. I'd come out without my key! And Mum and Dad weren't home! And Stallone wasn't trained to answer the door! And probably wouldn't even if he could!

This meant that I'd have to go down the alley a few doors along, climb up our back gate to unbolt it on the inside, race along our L-shaped garden path, whip the back door key out of the garden gnome's bottom, unlock the door, jump the *Wipe Your Feet* mat, swerve into the cloakroom, lift the toilet seat, and release myself to do the job in hand.

HOW COULD I DO ALL THAT BEFORE I BURST APART AT THE SEAMS?

As I reached the pavement (both hands on Willy Wonka duty now) I realised that I'd never make it round the back. Furthest I might get was our front garden a few steps away. I threw an arm round the lamppost by our gate to steady myself. Front garden, I thought. Mum'd been saying someone ought to water the plants. I'd be doing her a favour, wouldn't I? Yes. Good plan. I let go of the lamppost and started towards the gate, but after just one and a half steps I knew I wouldn't make even that.

And suddenly I was past caring.

I had to go!

Now!

I unzipped, whirled, and hosed the lamppost. While doing this (it went on for quite a while) I leaned on the post with my free hand and gasped my thanks at the sky.

It was one of those great moments.

The great moment ended when I removed my gaze from the clouds to watch the final drips drop and tuck myself neatly away again. On the way down my eyes caught the car that had silently pulled up two feet away while I was clocking heaven.

'You've made my day, son,' a policeman said, getting out. 'It's so rare to catch you young hooligans in the act.'

I was at the police station for over an hour before Dad came for me. He wasn't pleased to be summoned there. Last time he was there he said they didn't even give him a cup of tea to soothe his nerves, and he planned never to forgive them for that.* The overweight desk sergeant who smelt of garlic released me into his custody with a stern caution. Dad looked pretty shifty while this was occurring, like it was him being warned. As he

---

* See *The Snottle*, in which Jig's dad is mugged while out jogging – by joggers.

walked me much too rapidly to the car he told me that his heart had almost given out when the police phoned.

'Because you thought something terrible had happened to me?' I asked.

'No, because I thought they'd caught up with me.'

'Why, what've you done?'

'Well, there was that thing when I was school…'

'I don't think their records go back that far, Dad.'

'Don't you believe it. All human history's on the Internet, right back to the dawn of time. Jig, what were you thinking of, peeing in the street?'

'I was thinking what a relief it was.'

'But there are two toilets in our house.'

'I wasn't in the house, and I was desperate.'

'OK, but you must have felt it coming on.'

'It was kinda sudden.'

We got in the car and moved off. 'Your mother'll be livid when she hears,' Dad said.

'She doesn't know yet?'

'No. She was round at Janet's when they called. Last girlie chat before she goes on holiday.'

'Mum's going on holiday?'

'Janet. With Dawn. I'd only just got in myself. Just as well they didn't have my mobile number or I'd have missed the end of the match. Do you know, they have a seventy inch screen at The Kings Arms? Fantastic!'

'You won't tell her, will you?'

'Who? What?'

'Mum, about me being bundled off to the cop shop without a blanket over my head.'

'I'll have to. You know what your mother's like. Has to know every little detail of our private lives.'

'What's it worth?' I asked.

He glanced at me. 'What've you got?'

'Nothing. But you might need me to keep quiet for you sometime.'

He thought about this. Then nodded.

'OK. Deal.'

Later, in my room, I did a spot of thinking. My thinking went this way. The voice in the shell couldn't be heard by anyone but me and Stallone, though maybe Stallone could hear it because his ears weren't human, so, not counting him, why was I the only one who could hear it? That left me with a bunch of other questions. Well, four.

1. Who did the voice belong to?

2. Why didn't the voice know who it belonged to?

3. What was the voice doing in the shell in the first place?

4. If the shell came from Spain why didn't the voice speak in Spanish, or at least with a Spanish accent?

And then there was the frantic pee thing. The voice said it felt like it was floating. Could it be that this shell, and this one only, actually did hold the sound of the sea, and that the owner of the voice was on a stretch of water that was linked to the shell somehow? Also that whenever I heard the sea-sound a message zoomed to Section P of my brain, which texted my bladder, which sent an order to my dickory dock to splash my socks without delay while staring at clouds?

Hmm…

'Mum!' I shouted from the top of the stairs. 'I'm gonna take a shower!'

It was evening. My mother and father were

slumped in front of the gog-box as usual, which is why no one could hear me and I had to shout a second time, even louder.

'Mum! It's me! Your son! I want! To take! A shower!'

This time there was a distant crash. My mother bumping the coffee table as she lumbered to her feet. I waited until she flopped out to the hall like a porpoise with legs and stared up at me.

'Did you say shower?'

'Yeah, why, problem?'

'Has the moon turned blue or something?'

'Funny,' I said. 'I need a towel.'

'There are plenty in the airing cupboard.'

'I know, but which one? Last time you had a go at me for using the wrong one.'

'I can't remember that far back,' she said.

I frowned. 'Which *one*?'

'Use that bathtowel of your dad's. The big one with the stripper on. Do you want the instruction leaflet?'

'What instruction leaflet?'

'The one that tells you how to get into a shower and turn it on.'

'You should be on the stage,' I said. 'I'm wetting myself here.'

But I wasn't. That was why I wanted to take the shower. To listen to the shell and be able to stay put if I needed to go somewhere in double quick time.

I got the stripper towel out, admired it for a minute, then pressed the shower's On button inside the cubicle. The moment you press the button water shoots down from the big shower head and drenches your arm, so you have to make sure your arm's either bare, wearing a raincoat sleeve, or under an umbrella. (I had a T-shirt on, so it was only skin that got wet.) I closed the glass door with me outside to give the water a chance to warm up without me, stripped to the only suit I ever planned to own, and grabbed the shell. After leaning in and testing the water with a finger I stepped into the cubicle, closed the door, and slammed my back against the cold tiles to avoid the water.

Maybe I should explain that last part. Our shower is a power shower and I keep out of it as much as possible, as my mother gaily informs everyone she meets. I've tried telling her what it is about that shower that I don't like but she switches off the moment I start to explain, so let me write it down here. Maybe one day, when she's tucked up in a blanket in the Really Doddery Home, gawping open-mouthed at afternoon TV with sixteen others, I'll read this to her and she'll understand at last as she dribbles custard down her vest. According to my Kings and Queens of Sweden ruler, our shower cubicle is seventy-two centimetres in all directions but up. That's not huge. The only other power shower I've used was at the Next Family's, which I sampled four times in two days.* Unlike ours, that one was big enough to do a barn dance in with all your neighbours. Also unlike ours, the shower head was moveable. The head of our power shower is absolutely fixed, and as there's no room to hide from it, it beats down on your head the whole time. It might not be so bad if there was a dial to make the jet less fierce, but there isn't. It's Total Power or nothing. Even flattening yourself against the tiles and making yourself tile-thin, like I was trying to do now, the water still pummels any bits that stick out – and man, does it sting those bits! My mother doesn't appreciate any of this because (a) she's never used that shower, and (b) she has different bits. She

---

* Three of those showers were to get horse manure out of his hair, ears and nose. For the full disgusting story see *Kid Swap*.

'Something to wash yourself in. Theoretically. Wooh!'

'*What does wooh mean?*'

'It means that I...'

I didn't finish. I couldn't. I had an ultra-mighty need to piddle. But thanks to my forward planning I didn't have to squirm, cross my legs or grip myself to hold it in. I could relax and let go. And that's what I did. And out it swished, in a mad, mad gusharoonie.

'*I hear more water,*' the voice said.

'Yeah, me too. Look away, this is a private moment.'

'*Where would I look? I can't see a thing here, wherever here is.*'

The whooshing widdle was so powerful, so fierce, like...well, like from a flesh-and-blood power shower. I lodged the shell on the soap dish and watched the mighty torrent. There was even more this time than when I watered the lamppost. Where was it all *coming* from? I read somewhere that the average full-grown male body is about sixty per cent water. If that's right and I'm average and almost full-grown, about fifty per cent of my body must be made up of the stuff. As I stood watching, at least forty-five of my per cents gushed forth, smacked the tiles, bounced back, ran down my legs, and hiccupped merrily between my toes and down the drain.

I felt quite weak by the time I was all peed out. Not surprising really. With all that essential body fluid now on the outside of me, it's a wonder I was able to stand. Having a skeleton probably helped there.

'*The new water's stopped,*' said a small voice from the soap dish.

'Yeah, whew, 'bout time,' I answered.

'*You're very far away.*'

I took the shell off the soap dish. 'Better?'

'*Yes.*'

'You sound different,' I said.

'*I feel different. It's nice now.*'

'Why? Has something changed?'

'*I think so. It's all sort of...cosy.*'

'Cosy?'

'*Dark and quiet and floaty. Who are you?*'

'I already told you who I am.'

'*Did you? I forget.*'

'I'm Jiggy.'

'*Jiggy?*'

'McCue. And I really, really, *really* need a shower now, even this one, so if you'll excuse me...'

I put the shell back on the soap dish and thumped the On button.

Saturday. Afternoon. I'm in my room. Drawing. I do a lot of drawing. Always have. Drawing and writing. Well, obviously the writing. Jotting down all the stuff that's happened to me since I turned eleven. I've often wondered why everything started then. Other people seem to get past their eleventh birthday without being haunted by dead geese or having to wear evil underpants or getting lumbered with person-hating genies and so on. Not me. Not Jiggy McCue. When I write all this down I write it like I'm talking to someone, though I know that no one reads it. But as I sat there that Saturday afternoon drawing nothing in particular – doodling really – I got to wondering if my little sister would someday be interested in the stuff that happened to me when I was her age. Maybe, I thought, maybe when she's older she'll want to know about her big brother's crazy childhoo...

My drawing hand skidded to a halt.

'Holy jockstraps!'

If all this insane stuff started happening to me when I was eleven, would insane stuff also start happening to my sister when she hit the two ones? Was it something genetic that she would get, like I had, but which missed our parents and everyone else in our family since we fell out of the trees? Would it be just the two of us that...

'Holy migraines!'

My mum and dad were too boring and normal for anything really nutty to have happened to them, but how did I know I was the first in our family to get smacked with unnatural whammies? Maybe I had ancestors who'd suffered just as much. Ancestors on either Mum's side or Dad's who...

'Holy historical dramas!'

Maybe I was the first to get such things thrown at him *because* of Mum and Dad. Suppose I was unique because no one before me had received the deadly combination of my mother's and father's non-Levi genes. If that was it, then there was a good chance that Swoozie would also have those genes – and the problems they brought with them.

Poor kid. I was going to have to really look out for her. If she turned out like me, she was going to need all the help she could get from the older brother who'd been through all that junk before her!

Sunday. Peaceful Sunday. Except that it wasn't. The second and third halves of it anyway. Not being psychic, I didn't know before it happened that it was going to be one of the most memorable Sundays of my life. When I say 'one of the most memorable' what I mean is *the* most memorable. It started with a shout up the stairs from my mother. Nothing new there, she's always shouting for me when I'm in another room or on another floor, for no reason at all mostly. I ignored her, something I do quite a lot of.

It was just her, me and Stallone in the house. Dad was at a live footie match with most of the other no-brow males of the neighbourhood, including the Garretts, father and son. Pete used to hate football as much as me, but he'd changed lately. All of a sudden he'd rather watch numbered twits in shorts and tattoos slam balls though stretched hairnets than slope around with me, trashing the game. I blame body hair. Pete had been a slow starter in that department, but boy, had he caught up. Now, if I said to a stranger 'Meet my friend Pete, he's a gorilla,' the stranger would think I was only half joking.

It wasn't only Pete that'd changed. Eejit was talking in a voice almost as deep as his dad's, Ryan had joined a gym to get himself a four-pack, and I'd started acting cool when there were girls about. Girls. Most of them seem to glide through the puberty deal without changing much except in the chest area, and maybe the hip, but it affects some more dramatically. Like Angie. Angie had always been the most macho of the Musketeers, but suddenly she was wearing bras and doing things with her eyebrows. She always swore this would never happen to her, so I was pretty disappointed that she'd gone back on her word. She'd even started doing sleepovers, which she used to turn down flat. She'd been on one the night before the Sunday I'm talking about here, at some girl's she'd always sneered at for loving fluffy things. With Angie turning into a girl and Pete pinning up pictures of footballers, I was thinking that the end must be pretty nigh for the Musketeers. The famous battle cry might soon have to be changed to 'One for one and one for lunch,' with me the one. Sad.

Back to that Sunday afternoon. Like I said, it started with the shout from my mum that I ignored. I was in my room again, this time struggling to translate Pete Garrett's story about his grandpa's extra hole into English.

'Jiggy!'

There was something about the second shout that brought a frown to my chiselled features. I put my pen down, got up, went out to the landing, looked down the stairs. Mum stood at the bottom, holding on to the banister. She was standing in a puddle.

'My waters seem to have broken,' she said pathetically.

'Yeah? And that means...?'

'It means the baby's on the way.'

'No,' I said. 'She's not due for days yet.'

'Yes, well maybe she's like you. Keen to get into the world and start creating havoc. Call your dad, will you? And the taxi firm.'

'Taxi firm?'

'The number's on the fridge.'

'I've never called a taxi,' I said, suddenly nervous. (I'm not good on the phone to strangers.)

'Well here's where you start,' Mum said. 'And tell them to get a move on.'

'Who do I call first? Dad or the taxi firm?'

'Dad. I need him here.'

'He won't be pleased having to leave the match.'

'Jiggy! Hurry!'

I took the phone off the wall and buttoned Dad's number. It rang and rang, then rang some more, and finally a voice that wasn't his told me that the mobile I had called was switched off.

'He's switched off,' I said, going downstairs. Mum wasn't at the bottom any more, but Stallone was: sniffing the puddle she'd left behind.

I went into the kitchen. The fridge was a mass of fancy magnets with cards under them and I had to look for ages before I found one that looked like it belonged to a taxi firm. I went through to the living room. Mum was half-sitting, half-lying on the couch.

'Card here says Ever-Ready Taxis. Is that the one?'

'I don't know what they're called and I don't care what they're called,' she said, kind of irritably I thought. 'If it says taxi, ring them!'

'Would you do it?'

'Me? Jiggy, I'm going to have a baby!'

'Yeah, but you're good at multitasking, you're always saying.'

'Phone them!'

I went back to the kitchen and picked up the phone. Punched out the number on the card.

'*Hello,*' said a voice after three rings.

'Hello,' I replied. 'I need a taxi.'

'*This is Ever-Ready Taxis, your friendly local car service.*'

'Great. Could you send one to—'

'*I'm sorry, but we're closed for business at present due to strike action. Come back soon, won't you?*'

'Are you a recording?' I asked.

The line went dead. I hung up. Headed across the hall. Leaned into the living room.

'Ever-Ready Taxis isn't ready.'

'What do you mean?' Mum asked.

'They're closed.'

'Well ring the hospital.'

'The hospital? Do they do taxis?'

'They do ambulances! Ring them! Now!'

I traipsed back to the kitchen, snatched the phone, and called one of the few numbers I know by heart because my mother is forever pounding it into me in case of emergencies. This was starting to look like one of those, so it was a good number to know.

'*Which service do you require?*' a voice said.

'Are you human?' I asked it.

'*Human?*'

'OK, you are. I need an ambulance.'

'*I'll connect you to the General.*'

'General? No, I don't want the Army, I want the hospital.'

'*The General Hospital Ambulance Station. Putting you through now.*'

'Ah. Right. Terrific.'

There was a pause, then another voice.

'*I'm sorry, our services are currently overstretched*

due to industrial action and no one is available to process your call. Please ring back, or contact us through our website at www...'

I hung up. 'No ambulances!' I bawled, trying to sound calmer than I was starting to feel.

'Call Audrey!' Mum bawled back.

I sighed – there's no peace in our house – and dialled one of the few other numbers I knew by heart. No one picked up.

'No answer!' I shouted.

'Maybe she's in the garden and can't hear the phone!' Mum replied. 'Go over there! And don't stop to chat on the way!'

Talk about overreacting. But I went to the front door and legged it across the road. I rang Aud and Ollie's bell. No one came. I knocked. Still no one. I hammered. Nothing. I put my hands on the window and peered between them. You can see all the way through to their back garden by doing that. But there was no movement out there either. I thought Angie might have been in even if her mum wasn't, but no, so I reckoned she must still be at the fluff-loving friend's where she'd slept over.

'Now what?' I said aloud.

There was just one person left to try. Mum's only other friend in our street. I recrossed the road to the house next door and started up the Overtons' path, but halfway along it I remembered that Janet and Dawn had jetted off to Lanzarote in the middle of the night. I went back through their gate, then ours, up my path, into the house. I looked in the living room. Mum was now lying on the floor with her knees up and her hands clasped across Vesuvius (her former stomach).

'What are you doing down there?' I asked.

'Contractions. Where's Audrey?'

'She left no tracks.'

'What does that mean?'

'She's not in.'

Mum groaned. 'You'll have to call Cal P then.'

'Call what?'

'Cal P, the midwife.'

'Why's she called that?' I asked.

'Because she delivers babies,' Mum said.

'No, I mean...Cal-pee?'

'It's what she's called for short. Her number's – wooh! Heck! – in my bag.'

'Which is...?'

'Upstairs! Bedroom! My side of the bed!'

I charged upstairs. It wasn't easy keeping the trusty McCue cool with all that waters breaking stuff, and gasping on floors, and phoning hospitals and taxis, and going to neighbours, and fathers not being there when you need someone to stand behind. I went into Mum and Dad's room. Found the bag propped against her bedside table. I opened it and tossed female-type rubbish over my shoulder. There didn't seem to be anything else in there, but right at the bottom I saw a folded scrap of paper with my mother's scrawl on it. 'Cal P, midwife' it said, and a number. There was no phone in the bedroom, so I went out to the landing, unhooked the receiver and dialled.

'You have reached the voicemail of Calpurnia Pisonis. I can't come to the phone right now, but leave a message and I'll get back to you.'

Well, that explained the name, but knowing the midwife's proper name didn't help. Her picking up the phone, now that would have helped, but she hadn't, and all I could do was leave a message and hope she got it and did something about it before too many years tiptoed by.

225

'This is Peg McCue's son,' I said to the voicemail, and gave our address and added that my mother was on the carpet and could she come please because we kind of needed her.

When I hung up, I thought of going down to Mum, but went to my room instead and stood there for a minute, hoping that if I waited long enough there wouldn't be a problem any more. I do that sometimes if things get a tad heavy. Close my eyes and think of other things, or nothing at all, and hope it all works itself out by the time I open them again. Doesn't often happen, but sometimes it's all there is.

'*Hello? Are you there?*'

This came from the Spanish shell on my desk. I eared the shell. No sea sound for once.

'Hello,' I said.

'*Who's that?*' asked the voice.

'Me. Jiggy. What happened to the sea?'

'*It's gone.*'

'Gone? Gone where?'

'*It just went. It's like I'm being carried now.*'

'What do you mean, carried?'

'*Towards something.*'

'Well, good luck with that.' I had bigger worries than what was happening to a bodyless voice in a foreign seashell.

'*Who are you?*' the voice said then.

'Jiggy. I just said. Ever hear of a thing called short-term memory?'

'*I think I need you, Jiggy.*'

'Need me? What for?'

'*I don't know. Something's happening and I'm...*'

'You're what?'

'*I'm frightened.*'

'AAAAAAAAAAAAGGGGGH!'

This wasn't from the shell. It was from downstairs.

'Sorry, gotta go, catch ya later,' I said to the shell, and left the room in such a rush that I forgot to leave it behind. On my way downstairs I realised that I hadn't needed a piddly-dee after a chat with it either, but there was too much else to think about to wonder why.

I found Mum still on the living room floor, and Stallone was there too now, sitting near her, watching. Stallone doesn't sit near anyone usually. If I didn't know him better I might think he was a bit concerned.

'She's on her way, I know she is,' Mum gasped as I went in.

'She isn't,' I said. 'I had to leave a message.'

'I mean your sister.'

'My sister? I haven't got a…Oh, you mean…?'

'It shouldn't happen this suddenly, but…Jig, go and get a sheet and some towels from the airing cupboard, would you?'

I dumped the shell on the coffee table and ran back upstairs. Pregnant mothers are so demanding.

'Which sheet, which towels?' I yelled from the airing cupboard.

'Any!' Mum yelled back.

I grabbed a white sheet and a bunch of towels and jumped back downstairs two at a time.

'Not that one, it's one of my best,' Mum said of the sheet.

'You said any,' I reminded her.

'Any but a white one.'

I ran upstairs again and grabbed a blue one. Took it down.

'This OK?'

'Yes, yes. Quick now.' I started to spread the sheet over her. 'Under me, under me!' she said fiercely.

'Hey, take it easy,' I said.

'*You* take it easy!' she snapped. '*You* try having a baby!'

I let that one go and tucked the sheet under her as well as I could, which wasn't very well at all because she was built like Hellboy.

'Now get that booklet!' She was in one of her bossy moods.

'What booklet?'

'The one on the coffee table!'

I looked at the coffee table. At *Delivering for Dummies*, which I'd put the shell on top of. I lifted the shell and offered her the booklet.

'I don't want it,' she said.

'But you asked for it.'

'For you, not me. Turn to page five!'

I turned to page five wondering why. Saw all these instructions in big type like five-year-olds stare at with their mouths open. There were also drawings of a baby's head and a couple of things that made me wince.

'Why am I looking at this?'

'You're going to need it,' Mum said.

'What for?'

'Jiggy, why do you think?'

'I don't know, that's why I…'

I looked at her heaving stomach. I looked back at the drawings on page five. I looked at the stomach. At the drawings. While my eyes were darting back and forth, cogs turned slowly in my mind and rust fell off them. Finally, I found some words. Seven of them.

'I'll go outside and shout for help.'

'There's no time,' she said. 'It's up to you.'

'Me? Up to me? *Me*?' Suddenly I sounded like a talking mouse.

'You,' she said.

'No,' I said.

'Yes,' she said.

'Sorry,' I said. 'Got this urgent appointment up in my room with the door shut and my bed pushed against it.'

'Jig. You can do it. *Delivering for Dummies* will guide you.'

'Mother,' I said. 'I am not, repeat not, going down there.'

'Darling, it's nothing to be afraid of. It's where you came from, after all.'

'Yeah, fine, but I never had any plans to revisit it for old time's sake.'

'You must. There's no one else.'

'There's Stallone's. He's a bright cat.'

'Jiggy! She's nearly here! I can feel her! Get down there!'

'Mu-um...' I wailed pitifully.

'*Help me. Pleeeease!*'

This wasn't my mother. It was the shell on the coffee table. Stallone's fur and ears went up.

'*Heeeeelp!*' The shell again.

I glanced at Mum. Her eyes were shut tight. Even if she could hear the voice, her mind was on other things. So was mine. Things it didn't want to think about. Or do. But I had to do them, because like Mum said I was the only person available.

And do them I did. Yes. I did. With the free booklet from the clinic guiding me every step of the way. I won't describe it, if you don't mind. If I wrote it all down I'd have to relive it, and I prefer to save that for one of my future sessions on a psychiatrist's couch when we're trying to get to the bottom of why I'm such a screwed-up adult. Let's just say that when I hauled my baby sister into the world I did it mostly with my eyes buttoned, peering through half-closed lids at *Delivering for Dummies* for hints. Just as well it had pictures. I'd hate to have had to *read* about what I was doing.

But then it *was* done, and Mum was making these oh-my-god-thank-god-that's-over sort of noises while I stared and stared at this new little person in my hands. She had very fair hair that was all tangled and spiky, and these big smoky blue eyes that seemed to be trying to focus. And then they did focus. On me. And this itsy little frown appeared between them, like she was thinking, 'Have we met?'

I was still staring at my new sister and she was still staring at me and Mum was still gasping at the ceiling when I heard the front door open, and then Dad's voice, and someone else's. The someone else was Calpurnia Pisonis the midwife, who'd jumped into her car the moment she got my message. She came in and took over right away, wrapped Swoozie up and handed her to Mum, who immediately burst into tears. Dad just stood in the doorway in his football shirt with his jaw on his chest. His jaw and a number 2.

*

I worked it out that night in my room. The voice in the Spanish shell hadn't been a stranger's. It had been my new sister's. Swoozie's. The rest of what I worked out was this. Because we were so closely related there was a connection between Swooze and me even before she was born, but it was the kick I'd felt in our mother's tum three days earlier that had set up a direct line between us. The kick had sent a jolt all through my body to the shell in my opposite hand, which had then become a sort of communication device between us and given little unborn Suzie McCue a voice that only Stallone and I could hear. Don't ask me why Stallone could hear her. Maybe cats' ears can pick up stuff that most human ears can't.

Tiny unborn Suzie didn't know who she was, of course. Didn't even know her name yet. Or what was happening to her. All she knew was that she was floating, and she was too, but not on any sea. *On the water inside her mother's womb!* After the waters burst and she got closer and closer to being born, she had trouble holding on to what she'd learnt so far. She realised that something big was about to go down, though, and it scared her. By the time she popped out of her pod (like a brand-new pea) her little mind was absolutely empty again. Blank. All set to start from scratch.

I don't know who put it about – I didn't even tell Pete and Angie about it on the way to school – but the news reached Ranting Lane before we did next morning. When Registration was out of the way, Face-Ache told the class about me delivering my baby sister. Eejit Atkins wanted to know where I'd delivered her to, but everyone else was either speechless or wanting the gory details, which they didn't get.

Dakin asked me to stay behind while the rest went on to our first lesson of the day.

'I wanted to congratulate you in private,' he said with a smile. Yes, a smile. Dakin hardly ever smiles. 'Quite a thing you did there.'

I looked away. 'It was nothing.'

'Oh, don't be so modest, lad.'

'OK. Can I go now?'

He let me go, but not before cancelling the detention he'd given me on Friday. For once,

I didn't argue with him.

Pete and Angie were waiting for me outside the classroom.

'Why didn't you mention it?' Angie asked.

I shrugged. 'Slipped my mind.'

'Jig, how *could* you?' said Pete. He'd gone quite pale at the thought of what I'd done.

'No choice,' I said. 'Everyone else was on strike.'

There were questions all day long, even from kids I'd never spoken to before. A few girls patted me on the back and said stuff like 'Fantastic!', and Julia Frame gave me a tearful bear-hug that I thought I would never survive. Some of the boys leered and made the kind of remarks that should have got them a good thumping, but I wasn't in a thumping mood. Truth is, I was kind of happy, though it wouldn't have been cool to admit it. I had a sister! A *sister*! A very small sister called Suzie who I would have to stop calling Swoozie until she could speak and call herself that.

I couldn't wait to get home to her after school. Mum was there too, of course – and Dad, who was now on Paternity Leave, the skiver. Swoozie was asleep, all wrapped up and snug in a cot they bought weeks before from Argos. She looked so sweet, with her whacky all-over-the-place hair, her cute little Smartie of a nose, and her teensy thumb lying just in front of her mouth, like it was ready to get stuck in the moment it was needed.

'Hi, Swooze,' I whispered in her tiny ear.

She made a contented little sound which I like to think was her feeling good about Big Bruv being home.

Because Mum'd had this big event the day before, she said that Dad had to do the tea that night. Dad doesn't cook anything if he can help it, even toast, so he asked me to give him a hand.

'Hey, come on,' I said. 'I had a big event too.'

'Yours was nothing,' he said. 'My team was beaten into the ground by amateurs!'

'There's not much in,' Mum said, meaning food. 'I had intended to go shopping yesterday, but something came up.'

While she lounged on the couch like some queen, Dad and I trooped to the kitchen and peered in the freezer. Mum was right about there not being much choice.

'Chinese or pizza!' Dad bellowed.

'Chinese!' Mum bellowed back.

He took out the packet of Chinese food. The lettering on the front told us that we were going to have 'Sweet and Sour Chicken Balls in a Light and Crispy Batter with Soy Sauce'. Dad turned it over and started hunting for the instructions in English. 'Oh, I don't know about this,' he said, halfway through them.

I looked over his shoulder and also read the instructions.

'Place the sauce sachet on a microwaveable dish and cook on full power for 2 mins. Carefully remove the sachet from the microwave, cut along the top of the sachet, and pour the hot sauce over your balls.'

Dad looked at me. 'Pizza?'

'Perfect,' I said, shoving the Chinese back where it came from.

The pizza – mushroom, ham and red pepper – was a 'Family Size' one according to the guff, which as we all know means 'Enough For Three Small Relatives' when you remove the packaging. But we turned the oven to full to warm it up, gave it a couple of minutes, and slid the pizza in on an oven tray.

While we were standing around waiting for the pizza to cook, the front doorbell rang.

'Ignore it,' Dad whispered.

The bell rang again. And again. Began to sound like it would go on forever.

'They'll go away eventually,' said Dad, crossing his fingers.

The bell rang once more. Then twice more.

'Will someone please *get* that?!' Mum screeched from the living room.

I shrugged at my father. The boss had spoken. I went out to the hall and opened the door.

'Hello, er...Jiggy?'

On the step, with suitcases, were the tanned pensioners last seen being driven at breakneck speed to a place that didn't exist. Behind them in the street a small red hatchback zoomed off like a getaway car.

Dad came out of the kitchen. When he saw who it was he went pale. 'You!' he said.

'Us,' said Archie. 'That bloody train of yours never turned up.'

'But that was Thursday!'

'Yeah. Four days of hell.'

'You haven't been there all this time?'

'Yep. Dozing on benches, eating nothing but chocolate and nuts, drinking fizzy drinks, and we had to smash our way into the machine to get those. Damn thing wouldn't accept Spanish coins.'

'But...why are you here?'

'A car eventually stopped at the station. Don't know what the driver wanted, didn't care, first car we'd seen since yours, so we persuaded him to drive us here.'

'How?' Dad said. 'At gunpoint?'

'Are we going to be allowed in,' Bella said, 'or do we have to stay on the step all night?'

Dad's jaw was like an iron replica as he tried to make up his mind which answer to give to that. The decision was made for him when Bella pushed past him. Archie followed her in.

'Get the bags, Mervin,' he said.

'Marvin,' said Bella.

'Melvin,' said I.

'Mel,' said Dad through his teeth.

He brought their cases in and kicked the door closed, like he hated it, and glared at me for opening it. I mouthed a 'Sorry' at him, but it was too late, they were in, with their cases.

'Who was that at the door?' (Mum's disembodied voice from the Queen's Couch in the living room.)

'No one *invited*!' Dad yelled, obviously past caring if he offended them. Not that they would have been. My grandparents have skin like concrete rhinoceroses.

Mum stared with a mixture of surprise and horror when her parents strolled in.

'Mum! Dad!'

'They just stopped off on their way home,' my father snapped. Then he turned to his in-laws nervously. 'Didn't you?'

'That's right,' said Archie. 'According to the young fella who drove us here – shocking driver, wouldn't listen when I told him what he was doing wrong – the strikes that affect transport end tonight. We'll start back in the morning.'

Dad gripped something. My shoulder. 'The morning?'

'Well, there's no way of getting home today,' said Bella.

'I'll book you a hotel room!' Dad said, starting back to the kitchen.

'Oh, we don't need to go to that expense,' said Archie. 'We'll use your spare room.'

My father lurched to a halt. 'We haven't got a spare room.'

'Yes, you have. You cleared it out. You showed it to us.'

'That's Suzie's,' Mum said.

'Suzie?' said Bella.

Mum immediately went all melty round the eyes. She got up and led her mother to the little cot in the corner.

'Whose is that?' Bella asked, looking into it.

'Mine. Ours.'

'Yours? But it's not due yet, is it?'

'She arrived early. Yesterday.'

'Without warning,' Dad muttered. 'Like certain other members of her family.'

'Sweet,' said Bella, turning away. Never much of a baby person, my grandmother, or any kind of child person. Archie isn't either, which could be why they've never been completely sure of my name.

241

'New kid, eh?' Archie said, not bothering to go and look in the cot.

'Yeah, another ungrateful mouth to feed,' said Dad, glancing at me.

'But it doesn't sleep in its nursery yet, does it?'

'She's not an it, she's a girl,' I muttered.

'There are no beds in there,' Dad said to Archie.

'We'll doss on the floor,' Archie said. 'Got used to sleeping rough since you dumped us at that hole of a station. Is that food I can smell? We're starving!'

What he could smell was burning.

'The pizza!' said Dad.

Archie slapped his lips. 'Pizza! Just the ticket!'

Dad and I elbowed one another to be first to the kitchen. 'Should it do this quickly?' he asked as I put on floral oven gloves and hauled the tray out of the oven along with a faceful of smoke.

'Not if you remember to turn the dial down from furnace heat, like we didn't,' I said.

'It doesn't look burnt,' said Dad.

It didn't either. And it wasn't. But something was. I lifted the edge of the pizza.

'We forgot the polystyrene base,' I said.

'Polystyrene base?'

'You're supposed to take the pizza off it before putting it in the oven. We didn't, and the heat's welded it to the crust.'

I tried separating the polystyrene from the pizza. It wouldn't shift. It was part of it now.

'Wonderful,' said Dad. 'Not only is there not enough for five, but it's inedible.'

'There's always the Chinese chicken balls,' I suggested.

He shook his head. 'Not enough of them for five either.'

'So maybe we'd better ring for a takeaway.'

'Waste hard-earned money on those two?' he said. 'No chance.'

'What then?'

'Nothing for it. You, me and Mum'll have to divide up the chicken balls and they'll have the pizza.'

'What about the polystyrene?'

He narrowed his eyes. 'Maybe it'll choke them.'

When we'd cooked the chicken balls (just twelve small ones between the three of us) and done that thing with the sauce, we carried the five plates into the dining room. Mum and her parents were already at the table. Archie was gripping his knife and fork in anticipation. Mum asked where the Chinese rice was.

'Rice?' said Dad.

'From the freezer.'

'We didn't see any rice.'

'Well it's there.'

We went to look. The bag of frozen Chinese rice was hiding right at the back where no one but a mother would see it. Well, too late now. We went back to our riceless chicken balls.

My grandparents were already well into the pizza. Talk about manners. They were so starved of what looked like proper food that they didn't seem to notice either the polystyrene or that they had so much more on their plates than Mum, Dad and me. They had quite a struggle sawing through the base, but didn't even complain about that. Archie tossed an especially tough bit of crust in Stallone's direction, obviously not knowing that he doesn't like having food chucked at him. Stall stalked across to the leg of the throwee and dug his claws into it. This didn't go down too well with the leg's owner, though the McCue branch of the family were quite amused. Even Swoozie chuckled in her sleep.

Listening to my brand-new sister's sweet little gurgles and looking at that bristling warrior cat snarling at the grandfather who had trouble remembering his son-in-law and grandson's names, I realised something. What I realised was that if Pete and Angie ever decided that they'd outgrown the Musketeers and handed in their non-existent membership cards, there were two others who could take their place. Swoozie and Stallone. All right, one of them was a cat and the other was a baby, but it would still make us three against the world, and that was a comforting thought. Smiling at this, I tilted my glass of SmartSave Cola at Stallone and Swoozie and said, 'One for all and all for lunch!'

'Lunch?' Mum said. 'It's not lunchtime.'

'I know. But I thought someone should make some sort of toast, this being a special occasion and all.'

Dad scowled. Yesterday was special, the scowl said. Today's a pain in the behind.

When the three chicken ball plates were down to one last ball apiece, my mother remembered that there was something else we could nibble on. Peas, freshly shelled last Thursday. Dad said no thanks, he wasn't a pea person, but that he'd get some for her if she liked. Mum said she'd do without because peas are fattening. (She'd gone on a crash diet seconds after the birth.)

'Jiggy?' she said.

I looked up from my final chicken ball, which I'd sliced in half to make it stretch. 'What?'

'You'd like some peas, wouldn't you?'

'No.'

'No? But when we were shelling them the other day you said how delicious they were.'

'They were. But since then I've had enough pees to last me two lifetimes.'

I raised my glass again, to everyone this time, for no other reason than that I felt like it.

'One for all and all for lunch?'

Stallone snarled. Swoozie burped.

It was a good moment.

One of the best.

Almost as good as peeing against a lamppost in the street when you're too desperate to hold it in a second longer.

Brother Jiggy (McCue)

Look out for more JiGGY in 2010!

RUDiE
DuDiE

A new drama teacher arrives at Ranting Lane School.
Is Jiggy really going to have to play Bottom in the
school production of *A Midsummer Night's Dream?*

And introducing a brand-new series...

JiGGY'S
GENES

...in which we meet a whole host of Jiggy's ancestors
and discover that, through centuries past,
there have *always* been Jiggy McCues!

Don't miss the first book,

JiGGY'S
MiGHTY
BALLS

where we meet a 13th century Jiggy...

Don't miss
the next exciting
JIGGY adventure...

COMING 2010

TURN THE PAGE
TO READ THE BEGINNING...

CHAPTER ONE

Teachers should be banned. Some of them at least. The ones who shout all the time for no reason. The ones whose middle name is Detention. The ones who put a hex on you that makes you drop your pants and flash your bum in public places. Yes, I know the last of these is a bit unusual. In your life anyway. But you're not Jiggy McCue. Jiggyworld seems to be ruled by nutters like that.

The teacher who made me flash my basement cheeks was new at Ranting Lane. Her name was Ms Mooney. Our first sight of her was on day one of the new school year, when the entire school was jammed into the main hall to be welcomed, warned about misbehaving and introduced to her from the stage. She was unlike any teacher we ever saw. She had this tragic fright-wig-type hair (orange, obviously dyed) and a nose that flipped up at the end, and she wore very jazzy clothes that didn't match anything in sight, and all these bangles that rattled, and a clunky necklace that looked like bits of coloured rock. She was also shorter than every boy over twelve except Eejit Atkins, though we didn't realise it till our first lesson with her. This occurred the first Wednesday afternoon of term, in the gym. Her lessons were to take place there because we would need space for them, apparently. Ms Mooney was taking us for Drama.

Drama! Like I needed more of it in my life!

We soon learned when we met her nose to turned-up nose that this teacher wasn't one you could relax with. She had this quick, jerky way of moving, and she hardly ever smiled. But the most unrelaxing thing about her was her eyes. They were like twin black holes. There was something familiar about those eyes – and her expression when she stared – but if I'd seen her before I couldn't remember where.

One of the first things Ms Mooney got us to do when she came into the gym for our first lesson was tell her our names. Naturally, we tried the all-at-once routine first, but she shouted us down and told us to start again, one at a time, alphabetical order.

There was a bit of a slow start this time because Atkins is the second name in the register and he's not so hot at the alphabet. After him the name-giving went OK until I said mine and Miss stopped Angie Mint, who's next, and asked me to say it again. I was tempted to say 'Vladimir Putin' this time, but I played it straight because she was new. When she didn't seem to catch it the second time either, though, I said:

'Hey, Miss, if the old lugs are blocked I could bring in a bog plunger from home.'

This touch of good cheer was out half a split second before I noticed that she had bigger ears than normal. Her huge dangly earrings didn't do them any favours – in fact they drew your attention to them, but unfortunately they hadn't drawn mine soon enough. There were a few giggles and chuckles, but none from Ms Mooney.

'What sort of name's Jiggy?' she asked coldly.

I frowned. Ears or no ears, no one casts nasturtiums on my name, even teachers. 'What sort of name's Mooney?' I zapped back.

She narrowed her eyes. A blast of cold air whistled around my ears, but I tried not to show that she made me nervous. Show nervousness to a new teacher and they immediately think they have you where they want you instead of the other way round.

'You find my name amusing?' she said.

'Amusing?' I replied. 'No. Makes me think of mooning, that's all.'

'Mooning?'

'Dropping your nicks and dazzling strangers with your rear end.'

'I see.' She paused. Then she said: 'Jiggy, eh? I'll remember that.'

And she turned away, slowly and sort of deliberately, like she'd just made a threat. Our relationship had not got off to a perfect start.

When she'd got all our names, Ms Mooney told us what we were going to do in her lesson. A Shakespeare play. There were groans from at least half the class. One of the ones who didn't groan was Julia Frame.

'Brilliant!' she said, clapping her stupid hands. 'I love Shakespeare!'

But instead of turning a beam of teacherly delight on her, Miss flashed the black-hole orbs and said, in a voice straight out of the freezer: '*Do you now?*'

Julia didn't pick up on the ice, maybe because she was so thrilled about doing Willy-boy. 'Oo, yes, Miss. I know all his plays. Well, most of them. My dad's mad about them. He used to read them to me at bedtime!'

'Before they carted him off to the wack-house,' muttered Ryan.

'Quiet!' Ms M said. 'All of you!'

When most teachers say something like that it's about twenty minutes before we let silence take over, but there was something about this one that you didn't argue with...

Look out for
Rudie Dudie
in 2010 to find out what happens next!

READ ALL THE HiLARiOUS
JiGGY McCUE BOOKS!

All priced at £5.99

Orchard books are available from all good bookshops,
or can be ordered direct from the publisher:
Orchard Books, PO BOX 29, Douglas IM99 1BQ
Credit card orders please telephone 01624 836000 or fax 01624 837033
or visit our website: www.orchardbooks.co.uk
or email: bookshop@enterprise.net for details.

To order please quote title, author and ISBN and your full name and address.
Cheques and postal orders should be made payable to "Bookpost plc."
Postage and packing is FREE within the UK
(overseas customers should add £1.00 per book)

Prices and availability are subject to change.